5/16

Great Falls

Great Falls

STEVE WATKINS

CANDLEWICK PRESS

Copyright © 2016 by Steve Watkins

First edition 2016

Library of Congress Catalog Card Number 2015941691
ISBN 978-0-7636-7155-6

16 17 18 19 20 21 BVG 10 9 8 7 6 5 4 3 2 1

Printed in Berryville, VA, U.S.A.

This book was typeset in Minion Pro.

Candlewick Press
99 Dover Street
Somerville, Massachusetts 02144

visit us at www.candlewick.com

For Janet, and for the families of those who have served

Jeremy and I are stopped at that really long light on Route 3, stuck in a long line of cars waiting to turn and go into the mall. He's jumpy, agitated, checking all the mirrors constantly, even though we're sitting stone-still. A blue Chevy tries to nudge in front of us and Jeremy cusses and throws the truck in gear and cuts the guy off.

The guy, just somebody's dad in a white shirt and tie, glares at Jeremy and says something, but his window's rolled up — lucky for him. Jeremy smiles back, but it's not a real smile. It's the thin, almost painful-looking smile he gets when he's in the basement, cleaning his gun.

Please, asshole, I pray to the guy. *Just shut up. Just let it go.* I've already seen a couple of things like this escalate in the six weeks Jeremy's been back.

The light turns green and Jeremy lurches forward, nearly rear-ending the minivan in front of us, wanting to make sure the man in the blue Chevy doesn't get any more bright ideas about cutting in. As the minivan reaches the intersection, the light turns yellow and the driver brakes.

"Go, bitch!" Jeremy barks. "Just go already!"

But the minivan stops. The light turns red. And Jeremy fumes. His face is red and he's sweating and looking around even more anxiously than before. Mirrors. Windows. Mirrors again. He looks like a trapped animal, which, from the way we're boxed in by all these other cars and at this slow turn light, he sort of is. The blue Chevy is behind us now, the driver still glaring and running his mouth.

Jeremy fumbles with something under his seat.

"What's that?" I ask. "Did you drop something?"

He doesn't say, but I figure it out anyway: He's brought the damn gun with him. It's a 9mm, the same as his service pistol. He can't go a day without breaking it down, cleaning it — every last piece — then reassembling it. Now he's got it with him in the car. I shouldn't be surprised, but somehow I still am.

"You don't need that," I say, trying not to sound nervous.

"Need what?" he says, pretending.

"*That,*" I say, pointing.

Jeremy turns away. "You never know," he mutters, his

fingers playing over the steering wheel like it's a piano. There's no music on, though. He won't listen to music when he drives. But who knows? He could have a tune in his head he's playing along with. He's never still, I know that much.

The light seems stuck on red forever. A homeless guy who's been sitting against a concrete barrier in the median, not five feet from our car, pulls himself up off the curb. His hair is matted, a long nasty rope of dreads down his back. He's got a ragged beard and a deeply weathered face with obvious dirt in deep lines that are more like crevasses gouged into his cheeks and neck. His sign says VETERAN. SUPPORT THE TROOPS. NEED $ FOR MEDICINE. SEMPER FI.

I look and then look away, the way you're supposed to, but not Jeremy. He rolls down the window and calls the guy over. He pulls a ten out of his pocket and holds it out to the guy but doesn't let go when the guy reaches for it.

"Who were you with?" Jeremy asks.

The guy stares at him for a minute. I'm sure he can't help but notice Jeremy's buzz cut, what they call a high and tight, and knows Jeremy's active military.

"Marines," the guy rasps. "The Two-Five."

Jeremy grins for real. I haven't seen that look since I can't remember when. When I was a little kid, that's the face he wore all the time. But that was a long time ago.

"That's my unit," Jeremy says.

"No shit," the guy says. I don't think his hard, weathered face will let him grin back. He seems to be trying, though.

"Yeah, no shit," Jeremy says. "'Retreat Hell.'" It's the

3

Two-Five's motto. Jeremy taught me that when he first got assigned. The whole line, from back in World War I, is, "Retreat? Hell, we just got here."

The sun breaks out of the clouds and Jeremy has to squint. The homeless guy just nods. He's a lot older than Jeremy. He would have been in Vietnam probably.

The driver of the blue Chevy starts honking. The light has changed and the minivan in front of us is gone. Jeremy checks his rearview mirror but we don't move. Other horns are blaring behind us, too.

Jeremy lets go of the money.

"God bless you, brother," the homeless guy says.

Jeremy shrugs. "Semper fi."

The homeless guy nods and shuffles away toward the other cars. Everybody is honking like crazy now, the blue Chevy guy going at it nonstop, wanting to go through the intersection and not have to wait through yet another long red light.

Weirdly, Jeremy seems relaxed now. I don't know why. At least he's no longer reaching under the seat for his 9mm.

He lifts his arm out the window instead, gives the finger to the driver of the blue Chevy and to everybody else, puts the truck in gear, and drives slowly into the intersection as the light turns from yellow to red. Nobody else makes it through.

I wish he'd let me drive. I've had my license for nearly a year. I wish he'd talk to me about whatever's going on with him. I wish a lot of things.

4

We don't last long at the mall. We're there maybe ten minutes when Jeremy gets panicky or claustrophobic or whatever. Mom calls it hypervigilance and says he can't help it. She says he just needs time to adjust to being home.

All I know is Jeremy's eyes get really wide, and he keeps looking over his shoulder and all around us, checking the exits, making sure his back is to any wall he can find, which is hard to do in a mall. And then, before we even get to where we're going, he says we have to leave. *Now!*

So we do a forced march back to the car and haul ass as if somebody is chasing us.

We were just there to buy shoes.

2

I don't tell the Colonel what happened at the mall. He'd probably just shrug it off. "Cut him some slack, boy. He only just got home."

It wasn't always like this. He was always on Jeremy's ass before, from when Jeremy was a kid to all the way through high school. Only after Jeremy enlisted and got deployed did the Colonel start giving a shit. And once Jeremy got his medals — a Purple Heart and a Bronze Star after his third deployment — it was like he could do no wrong.

Sometimes, when he thinks no one is home, I can hear the Colonel in his study watching this YouTube video that a guy from Jeremy's unit posted. Jeremy was pissed at the guy for posting it, but it ended up going viral, so there wasn't much anybody could do about it.

The video is shot from Jeremy's helmet cam, so you don't see much of Jeremy except for his hands or legs or feet. It's like a real-life Call of Duty, the way you see what Jeremy sees as he's scrambling over rocks in this barren moonscape, panting and muttering "Shit, shit, shit, this is bad." The guy with him, Private First Class Tyler Atwell, Jeremy's radioman, is whimpering. They got separated from their unit and they're exposed on the side of a hill. Jeremy tells Atwell to shut it.

Then you hear *pock, pock, pock* — bullets hitting near them. The video goes blurry as Jeremy and Atwell dive for cover behind a rock that doesn't look big enough to hide a small dog.

Jeremy's turning this way and that so much, it's hard to follow. You do see an M16, and Jeremy's hands, and his shadow, firing back at the Taliban — not that you ever see any Taliban. Jeremy looks down, and Atwell is sprawled on the dirt, not moving at all.

The first time I saw the video I thought he was dead. Turns out he'd been hit in the face, bad. But he wasn't dead.

Jeremy keeps firing, and the rain of bullets keeps pouring down around him and Atwell, kicking up puffs of dirt on every side of them.

At some point Jeremy drags Atwell close to him behind their little rock. He pulls something out from inside his body armor, gauze or something, and presses it onto Atwell's face. You never actually see the wound, or the half of Atwell's face that got blown off—most of his cheek and eye socket and jaw on one side. The gauze quickly turns dark, but the helmet cam doesn't stay there. Jeremy is back kneeling behind the rock and shoulder-firing short bursts with his M16. And he's calling in for help on Atwell's radio, shouting his position over and over, and the coordinates for an air strike.

What's weird is how calm Jeremy is, though, even when he's shouting. The worse things get around him, the calmer he sounds. Telling them that Private First Class Atwell has been shot. Telling them where he thinks the Taliban are shooting from.

Something explodes just in front of their rock—it's an RPG—showering the helmet cam and Jeremy and Atwell with dirt and debris. The M16 goes flying and Jeremy goes down, too, but just for a second. Then he's scrambling on the ground, going after the weapon.

Once he retrieves it he scrambles back to Atwell and the meager protection of the rock. The dust clears away, and the helmet cam is fixed on Jeremy's hand, which is dripping blood. Jeremy seems to be counting the fingers on his left hand. One is missing. Out comes the gauze again, which he hastily wraps around his whole hand, stuffing a big wad tightly onto the bloody stump which is all that's left of his index finger.

Then he's back on the radio, and back shooting at the Taliban. He shakes Atwell. "Hold on, ass wipe!" he yells.

8

The helmet cam looks up at the sky, so blue that it hurts. And that's where the video stops.

Text appears over a dark screen on the YouTube version, filling in some of the blanks: how the batteries died on Jeremy's helmet cam, which is why the video ends where it does; how it took more than an hour for Jeremy and Atwell to be rescued by their unit; that Atwell survived his head wound, and Jeremy returned to active duty three days later; that he and Atwell both were awarded Purple Hearts. It says Jeremy also received a Bronze Star, which for some reason gets the Colonel worked up. He thinks Jeremy should have gotten the Silver Star. Or the Navy Cross.

"Maybe the Medal of Honor if he hadn't got separated from his unit," the Colonel once said, though from what I've read, you have to do a whole lot more than what Jeremy did to win the Medal of Honor. Or the Navy Cross, for that matter. Silver Star, maybe.

Not that there's anything to be ashamed of, winning the Bronze Star. All I know is Jeremy won't talk about it, and he won't show the medal to anybody. Not even me.

But the YouTube video leaves out a lot, things Jeremy told me one night when he was drunk: that Atwell was in a medically induced coma at Walter Reed for about a month, that he's lost all the sight in one eye and most of it in the other, and that they've already done half a dozen surgeries to repair what's left of his face, with more surgeries still to come.

The video also doesn't tell you that Jeremy's been staying

in our basement pretty much since coming back from his last deployment, and drinking a twelve-pack every evening to help him sleep. He spent all of two weeks at his and Annie's house across town, with their little girl, Nelly, and the new baby.

Nelly made too much noise, Jeremy said, and the baby, Greer, wouldn't stop crying, deep into the night. So Jeremy came over here, though he didn't want to be in his old bedroom with all his sports trophies and stuff. He wanted to be in the basement. Just temporarily, he said. Just until he could adjust.

The Colonel didn't ask how long, and Mom didn't say anything. Maybe she was glad to have Jeremy back under her roof, despite everything. Or maybe she just knows there's no use questioning the Colonel.

Jeremy disappears into his cave, not saying anything, when we get back from the mall. I grab my football gear from the laundry room and take off for practice.

We have a game tomorrow night. Coach has asked Jeremy to give a pregame talk in the locker room. I'm wondering if he'll actually show, especially after what just happened.

Jeremy went to my same high school, graduated eight years ago. They were state champions his senior year, with him playing wide receiver and cornerback. He probably could have played college ball. He got offers. They might not have been top schools or anything, but still.

He got in trouble instead. Blowing up mailboxes, of all things — on graduation night. With pot in the car when the police caught them.

And then he joined the Marines. It was the Colonel's orders.

Still, everybody in town loves Jeremy, or loves a certain idea they have about him, anyway. He can hardly walk down the street without someone stopping him and wanting to talk about the good old days or thanking him for his service and telling him what a hero he is.

3

It's Friday night and I'm in the locker room getting suited up for the game, pulling my shoulder pads on over a gray Marine T-shirt of Jeremy's, when my phone buzzes. It's him.

"Hey," I say. "You're late. Coach just asked when you're getting here. We're out on the field in half an hour."

Jeremy's still supposed to do that pregame pep talk or whatever.

"Yeah," he says. "I'm on my way."

The way he says it, I'm not so sure.

"So what's up?"

There's a long pause. Guys all around me are lacing up cleats, banging lockers, yelling at one another — already fired up. We're undefeated so far this season, so I don't know why Coach thinks we need Jeremy or anybody.

"Goddamn GPS isn't working," he says in a low voice. "Not sure where I am right now."

"You're lost?" I ask. This doesn't seem possible. We've lived here practically our whole lives.

"No," he says, clearly pissed off. "Yes. Sort of."

I don't get it. "Well just ask somebody for directions."

He ignores what I said. "There's a Walmart," he says. "A bunch of big-box stores."

I ask if he's been drinking.

"What are you, my fucking mother?" he shoots back.

"Sorry," I say, though I'm not. "So are you on a highway?" I ask.

"Yeah. Pulled over on the side. There's a RaceTrac gas station across the road. There's a Starbucks on this side. The Walmart's on this side, too."

"OK. Is there one of those big American Family Fitness places there, near the Walmart?"

He hesitates, and then says, "Yeah. Right over there."

I figure out where he is — south of town, where there's been a lot of retail development, though it's been there a lot longer than his latest deployment, so that can't explain why he doesn't know where he is, or why he's lost.

"Just turn around," I say. "Stay on Route One. You can probably make it here in ten minutes. You remember Coach asked you to talk to the team, right? You're supposed to be here?"

"Of course I remember," Jeremy snaps. Is he defensive because I'm questioning him, or because he's feeling guilty for forgetting?

"OK. See you in a while," I say, and hang up.

One of the few things I know about Jeremy's time in Iraq and Afghanistan — besides what I've learned from the YouTube video — is that he got blown up a couple of times during his first two deployments. He never gave any details, and since I couldn't see any scars and he wasn't ever in the hospital or anything, I figured that just meant stuff exploded near him or whatever but didn't hurt him.

Now I'm wondering if *blown up* doesn't mean something else: not being able to remember where you're going, or recognize where you are, even if you've been there a thousand times before.

Fifteen minutes later, Jeremy is standing in the locker room with us, everybody taped and ready for the game. I already got my shot of Toradol, so I'm feeling no pain, though I plan to inflict some on certain members of Courtland, who we're playing tonight and who kicked our ass last year.

Jeremy looks smaller in here than he does in real life, leaning against an empty locker, hands in his jeans pockets. Maybe it's because we're all in uniform, with helmets and pads and cleats. Maybe it's because he lost weight in the wars. Or maybe because he hardly eats now that he's back home.

Coach tells us to take a knee and then introduces him: Jeremy Dupree, All-District, All-State, captain of the state

14

championship team his senior year, *Captain* Jeremy Dupree, United States Marine Corps. He leaves out that Jeremy was always smart as shit, too — valedictorian, took so many dual-credit courses his senior year of high school that when the Marines sent him to college before officer training, it took him only a year to get his degree.

Coach is a stout, red-faced man, a former offensive guard at Virginia Tech back in the 1980s who played about ten minutes for the Philadelphia Eagles and never lets you forget it. He only cares about two things: football and model trains. Get him going on either subject and pretty soon his head explodes.

Jeremy pushes himself away from the locker and steps to the middle of the room.

"Coach asked me to talk to you gentlemen today," he says. "About winning."

You'd never know he was so lost just minutes before that he had to call his younger brother for help getting here.

"Well," he says. "There isn't any secret to it except one thing." He pauses and winks at me, as if I'm the only one in the room who's in on the big secret. Half the guys turn to look at me. Half just look bored.

"Forget what anybody says," Jeremy continues, "because it isn't heart, or willpower, or team chemistry, or any of that bullshit they tell you. It's superior firepower."

Guys look at one another with quizzical expressions. A couple look at me again. I don't give them anything back.

"We had the M1-A1 Abrams tank in the invasion,"

Jeremy says. "They had these ancient Russian pieces of shit. Had to come to a full stop before they could even fire."

Coach taps his watch. Jeremy nods but doesn't change the pace of his delivery. "We see their muzzle flashes about as soon as we cross over what they call the Line of Departure into the desert. Everybody's nervous, but then when their little turd bombs bounce off the Abramses, which are about the most heavily armored tanks in the history of modern warfare, we start laughing. And we keep on laughing when our guys unload a bunch of Sabot rounds on the Iraqis before they can throw their tanks back in gear and haul ass."

He pauses, looking casually around the room, pulling rank on everybody just through his eyes. Guys sit up straighter, though most probably don't know what the hell he's talking about.

"Sabot rounds carry depleted uranium rods," he says. "They're armor-piercing shells. So they punch right through those piece-of-shit Russian tanks. Through and through shots. Suck out everything and everybody as they exit — from the kinetic force or whatever. Rip their tank operators apart. Literally. At the molecular level."

Jeremy sticks his hands back in his jeans pockets and shakes his head, remembering. "That was some sick shit," he says. Then he nods at Coach again, and leaves.

Nobody moves for about a minute, until Darryl Shook, a linebacker, like me, whistles. "The hell was that all about?"

Everybody laughs. Somebody else says, "Hey, Coach,

can we get some of those Sabot rounds and unleash hell on Courtland?"

Coach's face is twice as dark as its usual red. He doesn't acknowledge the comments, just barks out a quick pregame prayer—"God grant us this victory, we humbly beseech Thee"—then we go charging out of the locker room, down the tunnel, and onto the field.

Darryl runs up beside me and says, "Your brother high or what?"

I throw an elbow that catches him on his chin strap and sends him staggering to the turf. I keep running. Somebody else stops to help him up. A few minutes later during warm-ups I see him. He's on the bench with the trainer, holding an ice pack to his jaw, with a big butterfly bandage on his chin. I jog over. He flinches. "Jesus, Shane. What'd you do that for?"

I tap his shoulder pads. "You OK?"

He spits out blood. "Asshole."

Jeremy is sitting near the end zone in a deserted section of bleachers, drinking something out of a paper bag. I wave when we line up for the opening kickoff, but he's not watching the game. The Colonel and Mom are in their usual seats near the fifty-yard line with the other parents and boosters. I wave to them, too — or to Mom anyway. She waves back.

The ref blows his whistle and we kick off. Courtland's speedy little return man finds the corner and sprints hard down the sideline, thinking he's going somewhere, until I demolish him.

4

I go over to Annie and Jeremy's house after the game. It's late but I know she'll be up. She always is. The baby, Greer, doesn't sleep much, so Annie is chronically sleep deprived, but she still has to get up early most days for her morning shifts at the hospital. Nelly has preschool, and Mom watches Greer some.

The porch light is on when I get there, and the door is unlocked, which I wish Annie wouldn't do. She's always happy to see me, and I've been coming over after my games the past couple of weeks, since Jeremy moved out.

"Hey, Annie," I say, pushing the door open and stepping into the front room.

"Hey, Shane," she whispers. She's lying on the sofa with Greer conked out on top of her. "I just finished nursing her. She's asleep." Annie sounds excited. Eleven is early for Greer. She'll probably wake up in a couple of hours, but Annie will take what she can get.

"Should I go?" I ask, not that I want to. I'm just being polite, offering to let Annie get some sleep, too.

"No," she says. "I want to hear all about the game. Let me see if I can get her in her crib first."

I help her ease up off the sofa, trying hard not to jostle Greer.

"Be right back," Annie says, all puffy cheeks and tired smile.

I sit on the couch after she disappears into Greer's bedroom. It's still warm and I let myself sink in. The Toradol has mostly worn off and I'm starting to feel all the hits I took — and gave — during the game. I had two sacks, six solo tackles, and half credit for that many more, though Courtland quit running to my side of the defense in the second half. Coach also had me in at fullback, which on our team is strictly a blocking position. He told me there was a college scout in the stands, but I never saw him, and he didn't come down to the locker room afterward. Probably because of the limited way Coach uses me on offense. Colleges want a fullback who can run the ball on short yardage situations and catch passes over the middle and catch screens in the backfield and run the option. Not just some asshole who can block.

And big as I am — six feet and two ten — I'm probably too small for anybody to recruit me at linebacker.

Annie comes back by way of the kitchen, holding a beer and an empty glass. She fills the glass halfway and hands it to me. "That's all you're getting," she says.

"I'm almost eighteen," I say, pretending to take the bottle.

She doesn't let go. "Drinking age is still twenty-one. Take it or leave it."

I take the glass. I don't even like beer. I just like the ritual.

"You and Jeremy weren't exactly twenty-one when you started," I say. Annie was two years behind Jeremy in school; they started dating during his senior year. She was with him and his friends that graduation night when he got in trouble, and she actually set off a couple of cherry bombs herself, though Jeremy lied to cover for her and she never got in trouble for it. I guess she was pretty wild back then, too — not that she'll admit to anything now.

"So how about a postmortem," Annie says, settling in beside me.

"What's that?"

She laughs. "It's an autopsy," she says. "But of the game."

"Oh," I say, feeling stupid, until she pats me on the arm. And then I start talking. I tell her we won, of course. Still undefeated. And then I tell her about running down Courtland's return man on the opening kickoff. She seems impressed, which makes me happy. Really, just about everything Annie says and does makes me happy. It's why I spend every Saturday over here doing chores, helping out around the house, watching the kids so she can take a nap, going with them out to lunch.

Annie turns serious when I get to the part about the Courtland trainer coming out on the field to check on the return man after the hard tackle. "He wasn't hurt, was he?" she asks. I love that about her, too — that she worries about everybody, even people she doesn't know.

I shake my head. "Just shook up. But he didn't want to have anything to do with me the rest of the game. Any side of the field I was on, he went the other way."

I go on for a while about other highlights of the game: a block I made that sprang our running back for a long touchdown run; a fumble recovery. Annie finishes her beer quickly and then has another, and then another after that. It's not long before she's yawning and slurring her words. Not that she's drunk. Drunk is how Jeremy gets: angry, cursing, blacking out, falling down, sleeping it off, waking up disoriented.

She finally gets around to asking about him.

"Was he there?" she asks.

I nod. "Yeah. For a while. Sitting by himself. But he left before halftime." I don't tell her about his "superior firepower" speech before the game, or about me taking out Darryl Shook for asking if Jeremy was high. I don't tell her about the gun under the car seat the day before either. I'm not sure why. It's not as if Annie hasn't seen and heard those sorts of things before, and worse.

"Was he drinking?"

I shrug. Of course he was, so why ask? She wants me to reassure her, so I do.

"He's just still adjusting to being home," I say, parroting the Colonel. "He'll come around."

She stands up suddenly, unsteady on her feet, and announces that she needs to go to bed, as if she just remembered. I help her to her bedroom. When we get there, she turns and puts her arms around me. She's so much smaller than I am. I'm always surprised by this, when she hugs me. I kiss the top of her head and smell the sweet scent of shampoo in her long brown hair.

She's crying softly now. I know the tears are for Jeremy. I just don't know what to do about them. One thing I do know is if I was Jeremy, I don't care what happened to me in the war, I wouldn't ever do anything to make Annie cry.

I go into Nelly's bedroom to check on her before I let myself out. She's kicked all the covers off, so I tuck her back in, even though she's wearing these little Marine footie pajamas, so probably isn't too cold. She's also hugging a giant Spiderman doll. Nelly's a total tomboy.

I check on Greer, too. She's still asleep in her crib. I make sure the front door is locked when I leave. I wonder where Jeremy is tonight — if he's home in the basement or out somewhere. He goes away sometimes, and I don't know where. None of us do. He might not even know himself.

5

The light's on in the garage when I get home. Jeremy's truck is parked on the street. The Colonel's car is in the driveway. I park Mom's car next to the Colonel's.

The automatic garage door is open, and there's a homeless guy sitting in a lawn chair inside, drinking a can of beer. He's got a ragged duffel bag on the concrete floor next to him. His feet are propped up on a cooler. It takes me a second to recognize him. He's the vet from the turn lane at the mall — or the guy who claimed he was a vet anyway. A Marine.

He nods and says something, but it's unintelligible. He must see it on my face that I didn't understand, so he tries again, speaking harder, seriously slurring his words. "Heshinshide."

I figure it out. "He's inside? You mean Jeremy?"

The homeless man shakes his head, and then nods emphatically and jerks his thumb in the direction of the house. The garage opens into the kitchen. The door's closed.

"What are you doing here?" I ask, not that I expect an answer I'll be able to understand. He doesn't disappoint, but I don't ask him to repeat it. I just stand there and wait for Jeremy to come back from wherever he's gone.

Finally Jeremy stumbles out of the kitchen and down the three steps to the garage. "Shaney-boy!" he says, too loudly. He hands a new beer to the homeless vet and pops one open for himself, then drops down into a second lawn chair and lifts his beer toward me.

"Hail a conquering hero," he rasps. He picks something up off the garage floor — a half-smoked cigar, which he relights. The homeless guy is holding one, too, unlit. "Boy's a goddamn gridiron star," Jeremy says, elbowing him. I can't tell if he's making fun of me or just drunk.

"How goes it, bud?" he asks me. "Been out celebrating the great victory? Damn fine performance tonight. What I saw of it. You just about killed that little dude on the opening kickoff. Well done."

He offers me his beer but I wave it off.

Jeremy kicks at a sleeping bag next to his lawn chair.

"This here is Staff Sergeant Louis Frank. Or Fank. Or Fink. Not exactly sure of the pronunciation, and he doesn't seem to be either."

Staff Sergeant Louis Frank/Fank/Fink doesn't pay any attention to us. He's busy draining his beer.

"Where'd you find him?" I ask. "He couldn't have still been out by the mall."

"Nah," Jeremy says. "He was downtown. Heading for the river. Probably has a camp down there. He had his duffel with him. It's supposed to rain tonight." It's all the explanation I know I'm going to get.

"The Colonel's going to kill you," I say.

Jeremy laughs. "Take a number, get in line."

"You don't care?"

"Not much. Besides, the Colonel loves me now. He'll probably thank me for helping out Sergeant Frank here. Buy us some more beer."

"No chance," I say.

Staff Sergeant Frank has passed out in his lawn chair. He's snoring softly. Jeremy tries to take the empty beer can out of his hand but the guy keeps a tight grip on it, even though he's asleep.

"Must be big into recycling," he says.

"Jeremy, are you OK?" I ask.

He blinks at me, like Sergeant Frank did when I first walked up. "Oh, yeah, sure," he says after a minute. "Except these fucking headaches. Nothing another twelve-pack won't fix, though."

He laughs. I don't. I tell him I went over to see Annie and the kids. I tell him Annie asked about him.

His face turns dark. "What did you tell her?"

"Nothing," I say. "Just that you came to the game. That you're, you know, working some things out, like Mom says. That you just need some time to adjust and all. Stuff she already knows."

Jeremy throws his beer can, bouncing it off the garage wall and sending it clattering across the floor. "I'm going over there tomorrow," he says. I'm not sure if I believe him, but I'm suddenly too tired to care. The Toradol's worn all the way off. It dulls pain and gives you a kind of buzz during the game and for a while after, but not forever.

"You staying out here with this guy?" I ask Jeremy, still sounding like Mom, I know. He lets it go this time.

"Why not?" Jeremy says. "I've slept in worse places."

I grunt. You could eat off the floor of the Colonel's garage. Once he finds out Jeremy had the homeless guy in here, he'll probably have us scrub the place down and fumigate it.

Sergeant Frank snores louder and loosens his grip on his beer. It clatters onto the concrete floor. The sound wakes him up. He looks around dully, then sags back into his lawn chair and closes his eyes, slipping into another world — probably the jungles of Vietnam — muttering and twitching in his restless sleep.

* * *

26

Jeremy and the homeless guy are both gone in the morning. I know this because the Colonel storms into my bedroom and turns on the overhead light. Then he kicks my bed and yells.

"Did you leave the garage door open last night? Goddamnit. Somebody stole the lawn mower!"

I struggle to sit up, too stiff and sore from the game to move very quickly.

"Well?" the Colonel demands. "What do you have to say for yourself? Think you play football and rules don't apply to you around here? Think somebody's supposed to go along behind you, locking up, putting things away? Don't think for a minute you're not paying for that mower!"

For a man so determined to get answers, the Colonel doesn't give me an opportunity to respond. That's the way it always is with him, once he has his mind set on an explanation about something that happened. Especially if it involves blaming me, now that Jeremy's turned into his Golden Boy and outranks him besides.

Even if I told the Colonel it was Jeremy who left the garage door open, and most likely—OK, definitely— Jeremy's homeless vet pal who stole the lawnmower and God knows what else, it wouldn't do any good. The Colonel would just accuse me of ducking responsibility for my stupid, thoughtless behavior. And he would still make me pay.

"Sorry," I say, lying back down and pulling the covers over my head. "I'll pay for it."

The Colonel kicks my bed again. "Goddamn right you'll pay for it!"

He storms out just as pissed off as he was when he came in. If he's not careful, he's going to have another coronary. Which I wouldn't mind at all.

6

Hours later, I finally drag myself out of bed, shower, take a fistful of ibuprofen, and scrounge whatever I can find to eat—leftovers, mostly, and coffee and eggs. I can hear the Colonel cursing to himself in the living room as he reads the paper and watches Fox News.

I open the door to the garage, not sure what I'm expecting to find. Jeremy won't be there, and he must have cleaned up all the beer cans and cigar butts, or else I would've gotten chewed out by the Colonel about all of that stuff, too. But the garage looks just like it always does. For a second I'm confused when I see the lawn mower, wondering if maybe

Jeremy got it back from Sergeant Frank somehow, or even if Sergeant Frank ended up feeling bad about stealing from us and brought it back himself. But then I realize that it's not the same lawn mower. The Colonel has already gone out and bought a new one, even though it's October and there won't be any need to mow until the spring. But that's just how he is.

Mom must be out somewhere, because her car is gone. I don't have to go to work until this afternoon — I do afternoon shifts on the weekends at a Wawa gas station out by the interstate — so I head over to Annie's. I told her I would rake the yard, even though Jeremy's home now, and so he should probably do it. But we both knew that wasn't very likely.

I have to ride my bike, since there's no way in hell the Colonel would ever let me borrow his car. I've never even bothered to ask.

Jeremy's truck is sitting on the street in front of their house when I get there, and I think about turning around and heading home. But even if Jeremy is here, it's not like he's going to be out doing yard work later.

The door is locked, so I knock softly and Nelly lets me in. She says, "Hi, Uncle Shane," and then leads me over to the couch in front of the TV. I sit down next to her.

"Where is everybody?" I ask. Before Nelly can answer, I hear Greer crying in the back of the house.

"They're in bed," Nelly says. She has a bowl of dry Frosted Flakes next to her, and I grab a handful.

"When did your daddy get here?"

"I don't know," she says, eyes fixed on the TV. "He was just here."

"Did you see him?"

"Uh-huh. Mommy told me to watch TV and let him be asleep."

I nod. "Probably a good idea. You wait here. I'll be right back."

I go into Greer's room. She's standing in her crib, holding on to the bars. Tears streak down her face, but she doesn't seem too terribly upset. I pick her up and feel right away that she needs a new diaper. I'm an expert at changing babies — I got plenty of practice on Nelly during Jeremy's first deployment, and I changed Greer more times than I can count during his last deployment — so it doesn't take me but a minute to get her cleaned up. I grab a clean Onesie from the dresser and change her clothes, too.

I wonder if anybody else on the football team even knows what a Onesie is.

I stick her in the BabyBjörn and take her with me and Nelly outside to start raking. Nelly has a little toy rake I bought her with my Wawa money, and every time I rake a pile of leaves, she wades in and toy-rakes it into a bunch of smaller piles. Then she jumps from pile to pile, scattering all the leaves. Greer whimpers — it's probably not the most comfortable thing in the world to be strapped to your rather large uncle's chest while he's raking leaves — and I give her a bottle of formula Annie had in the refrigerator. She fusses at first. Babies don't like cold bottles. But she's hungry, so she ends up drinking it all.

I must look ridiculous right now, and just hope nobody I know drives by and sees me. I'd never hear the end of it in the locker room.

I'm just about through with the front yard, though Nelly is gaining on me, when Annie comes out and sits on the front steps, both hands cradling a mug of hot coffee, a baby blanket over her shoulder. Wisps of steam rise up to her face in the crisp morning air. It occurs to me now that it never rained last night — which was the reason Jeremy gave for bringing Sergeant Frank home to the garage. I wonder if it was ever even supposed to rain.

Annie presses the mug to her forehead, the way you do when you wake up with a headache. I drop the rake and sit next to her.

"Hey," I say. "I have somebody here who wants to see you."

Greer is reaching around, trying to twist herself out of the BabyBjörn to get to Annie. I unhook the straps. Annie sets her mug down and takes the baby. "Thanks."

Nelly waves her little rake from the yard, where she's messed up yet another one of my leaf piles. I'm going to have to rake them all over again to bag them up later. "Hi, Mommy!"

Annie smiles a strained smile back. "Hi, sweetie." She shifts the baby blanket to cover herself as she lifts her shirt so Greer can nurse.

"I did all this!" Nelly yells. "Uncle Shane helped me!"

"That's great, sweetie," Annie says, adjusting something under the baby blanket. Greer squirms and then settles down to business.

I slip the BabyBjörn loops off my shoulders and set it down on the steps. "Jeremy inside?"

Annie nods. "He came over a couple of hours after you left. I think. I was asleep." She rocks Greer, readjusts the blanket. I smile at Nelly, still working hard dividing up the leaf piles.

"He had one of his nightmares," Annie continues. "I think it was around four. He took something. I'm not sure how long he was up, or when he crashed." There's a deep weariness to Annie's voice as she says all this, like even speaking the words exhausts her, and like nursing the baby as well is leaving her depleted, nearly empty. She slumps back on the steps. Greer keeps nursing.

"Don't you have to go to work today?" I ask, though it's Saturday. But I'm pretty sure she told me she had pulled weekend shifts this week.

"Called in sick," she says. "I didn't get much sleep last night either." She punches me lightly on the arm. "And you, you little jerk. You let me drink three beers. I never drink three beers. I'm usually one and done."

"Sorry," I say, laughing back, glad the conversation, and I hope the morning, is taking a lighter turn. "I didn't know I was supposed to be on beer patrol."

"Oh, yeah," Annie says, lifting up Greer. "You were

supposed to be the designated driver." Greer has a runny nose and wipes it on Annie's shoulder. Annie doesn't even bother to clean it off. Between her own two kids and working in the pediatric ICU at the hospital, she's used to that sort of thing. It still grosses me out, though.

I point out that we weren't driving anywhere last night, just sitting on the couch.

"Good thing, too," Annie says. Then she changes the subject again. "Did you see if Nelly ate anything? I saw her cereal bowl."

"That was all. Just the dry Frosted Flakes. She has a nice sugar buzz going."

We both watch Nelly for a while, zooming from leaf pile to leaf pile with her little rake, sticking to the job a lot longer than I would ever have expected from a three-year-old. Not that I know much about kids. I just like them is all. Especially Annie and Jeremy's.

"Probably should get her some real food," Annie says after a few quiet moments. "Probably should feed you something, too. Get you some energy to redo all that raking Nelly has managed to undo for you."

Sunlight filters through an elm that sits just off the front steps. It still has half its leaves. I'll need to come back next weekend and rake all over again. Unless Jeremy stays around and does it himself. "How much am I getting paid for this again?" I ask. "I forget."

Annie hands me the baby. "All the wet diapers you can change. You get to keep them."

She calls to Nelly that it's time to come in the house for breakfast. I pat Greer's butt to see how soggy it is. Hard to believe a little baby can pee so much.

"Remember to be really quiet when we go inside," Annie says to Nelly. I can hear the worry return to her voice. "We don't want to wake up Daddy."

7

Jeremy gives me money to pay for the lawn mower, but he doesn't offer to tell the Colonel that it was his fault, that he brought a homeless guy to the house and left him alone in the garage. I don't say anything either.

That night at dinner, Mom tries — in her cautious way — to talk the Colonel out of taking the money when I hand it to him. "Ted, honey, do you think maybe instead of paying for it with his savings we could have Shane work off the debt? He's putting away for college, and we do need some things done around the house and in the yard. . . ."

We're sitting at the dinner table, just the three of us. Jeremy's still over with Annie and the kids. I just got back from my shift at Wawa.

The Colonel lays his fork and knife carefully down on his plate, crossing them exactly in the middle. He rubs his temples, and Mom looks down at her plate. We all know what's coming.

"Chores are a responsibility of living in this house," he says evenly, not mad yet but never far from it. "Do you get paid for doing chores, Diane? Did you get paid for making this dinner? Did I get paid for taking time out of my Saturday to drive down to Home Depot to buy a new mower? Did you know, Diane, did you *know* that I also found beer cans in the garage? I didn't tell you about that, and do you want to know why? Because living with you has made me soft. It has made your younger son soft. It made your older son soft until the Corps saved him from himself. Is that really what you want, what you think is the best way to raise your son — to be going along behind him like you're his nanny, cleaning up all his messes? Is it? Will we be bailing him out his whole life? Is that the plan now? For god's sake, try using some sense here. You break it, you bought it. It's as simple as that. He left the garage door open, someone stole the lawn mower, he pays, end of story. He came into *my* house, he took *my* beer, he didn't even bother to hide the fact. You worry that I'm too hard on him and his brother, so I go soft, too. I let things slide. And look what it goddamn gets me. Now you want to let everything go. You want him to just skate free. Maybe do a load of laundry. Maybe coil up the garden hose, or walk outside and get the mail. Well, it's not going to happen. He *will* pay for that mower. He *will* pay for the beer he stole. What is more, he'll be grounded for the next two weeks, and do chores every day when he comes home from school. And if anything like this ever happens again, he will no longer be allowed to play football. As far as I'm concerned, it's a waste of time anyway. He isn't good enough to make it at the next level. He could be asking for more hours at work, studying more, saving more money — money that he will hopefully manage to actually hang on to and not burn through, paying for his irresponsible actions. He *will* be held accountable, I promise you that. In this house, he will *not* be allowed to go soft. Do you understand all this, Diane?"

The Colonel's face is purple, but that's all. He still sits stiffly, not moving his hands, not gesturing wildly or anything like that. Mom has long since retreated inside herself, the way she always does when the Colonel launches into one his rants. I just sit here, too, knowing there's nothing I can say, nothing anybody can say, that will do anything but piss him off even more. He's such a goddamn cliché — the hard-ass ex-military stepdad. I'm practically embarrassed for him.

"I asked you a direct question, Diane," he snaps. "I expect an answer."

Mom nods. "Yes, Ted. Of course. I see your point." Her voice is flat, and faint, coming from so far away, wherever it is she travels to when the Colonel goes off on her. I've gotten pretty good at doing that, too.

Jeremy always sucked at it.

The Colonel hasn't looked at me the whole time this has been going on. He does that sometimes, too — erases you even when you're sitting right there. Tomorrow he might buy Mom some flowers, or take her out to dinner, or do something else nice. He's always been a big one for the grand gesture. Or he might not. It all depends, though I'm never quite sure on what. For the rest of tonight Mom will be silent and go to bed early while the Colonel stays up watching sports on television. He might order me to sit down and watch with him, or he might let me stay in my bedroom if I tell him I have to do homework, even though it's Saturday and who the hell does homework on a Saturday? But I'm grounded now, which means no hanging out with my friends or going over to check on Annie. Not that I do that much hanging out anyway. Though I guess I can always wait until the Colonel goes to bed and sneak out of the house the same way Jeremy used to do.

Mom usually leaves the room when the Colonel decides to go off on me directly. She'll make up an excuse to come find me later, though. She'll ask if I can help her with the crossword, or if I'll taste these cookies she just made, to see if she left something out or if they're OK. She'll sit on my bed and we'll talk — about school, about the team, about nothing — until she convinces herself that I'm not too upset about the Colonel, and about her never standing up for me. She didn't get to do that much for Jeremy. He would either mouth off back to the Colonel, and get hit, or else he would run away. Sometimes both.

I read that in Vietnam the grunts sometimes killed their

own officers — for putting them in unnecessarily dangerous situations, for getting their friends killed with stupid orders, for ragging on them too much. They called it *fragging*.

Sometimes, like tonight, I think that if it takes too long for another heart attack to kill the Colonel, I might have to borrow Jeremy's gun and frag the son of a bitch myself.

The Colonel isn't our actual dad. He's not an actual colonel either, just another peacetime Marine noncom who never had a rifle fired at him in anger. That's what Jeremy told me; I never asked. I'm not sure why we started calling him the Colonel back when we were little. He made sergeant but never went any further. Jeremy outranks him by a lot. The Colonel's biggest claim to fame was service in the Grenada conflict back in the eighties, which was basically America stomping the shit out of some communists who pulled off a coup in this little island country in the Caribbean that nobody had ever heard of — before or since. The communists didn't even have an actual army. The whole war took about ten minutes. And the Colonel wasn't even in the actual conflict. He was what Jeremy calls a REMF: a Rear Echelon Mother Fucker.

He was our real dad's squad leader at Camp Pendleton in California. He met Mom after our real dad got killed in a Jeep accident. Not in any war. Not even in Grenada, where more people were killed when we accidentally bombed a mental hospital than in any battle. He was just driving somewhere. Jeremy said he hit an antelope, but I think that's just a story he made up to make it sound dramatic or exotic or something. Our real dad flipped his Jeep and he died. That's all I know for sure.

Mom was a young widow with an eight-year-old and a one-year-old. She didn't have any family to speak of, just some cousins in Arizona. The Colonel was nice to her. At first anyway. Bringing over takeout. Helping her with all the paperwork to get a widow's pension. Lending her money to go back to school. Bringing over toys for Jeremy and diapers for me. The Colonel said he would take care of her, and us, and she believed him. What else was she going to do? They got married six months after our real dad died.

Then the Colonel changed. That's how Jeremy remembers it anyway: at first the Colonel doted on Mom and on us, then he started yelling and throwing things and sometimes breaking stuff. He never hit Mom, but he was always giving her orders and criticizing the way she carried them out. I remember always being afraid of him, and Jeremy always letting me in bed with him when I was afraid. But I wasn't scared about bad things happening to me, exactly. It was always Mom and Jeremy I was worried about — Mom because she usually took the brunt of the Colonel's anger, and Jeremy because he was always talking back, as if daring the Colonel to hit a kid. I knew even back then that it was only a matter of time until it happened.

The Colonel mellowed some a couple of years ago, when he had his first heart attack. Not enough, though. We're hoping he has another, like I said.

41

8

Jeremy leaves on Sunday. He's supposed to be gone the next several days, leading field training for new officers at The Basic School out in the woods at Quantico, half an hour from here. He told me a little about what he does there — teaching leadership skills, and how to survive combat tours: stuff like Land Navigation, Communications, Combat Lifesaving, and something called Combat Hunter Mindset. There's no way to reach him — no phones, no Internet, nothing. I think he likes it that way.

Some of the guys on the team make a point of ignoring me on Monday, I guess still holding a grudge about me elbowing Darryl Shook in the face. It's actually kind of funny, like we're Amish and they're shunning me for whatever it is the Amish shun other Amish for: cutting their hair, getting drunk, refusing to grow a chin beard.

The silent treatment continues out on the practice field, where a couple of linemen block me from the huddle, and Dee Walker, our quarterback, mumbles the plays to the other guys in a way that I can't quite hear. I have to figure out from the way everybody lines up what the play is, and even then I mess up on a couple.

"What the living fuck is wrong with you, Dupree?" Coach yells when I go the wrong way on a counter draw and can't find anybody to block. I'm just standing out in the flat all alone, the play long gone in the other direction.

I throw up my hands. "Don't know, Coach." Clearly nobody told him anything about what I did Friday night, and I'm not about to break the code and say anything about them taking it out on me today and making me look bad.

Coach orders me to run stadium steps until my brain starts working right, and he doesn't let me stop for half an hour, until I'm starting to wonder if maybe somebody on the team *did* tell Coach about Friday night after all.

I apologize to Shook after practice. He's not ready to let it go, though. He just says, "Fuck you."

My cell phone rings in the middle of the night.

It's Jeremy.

"Need you to come get me," he says. "They won't let me have the truck."

"Come get you from where?" I ask, shaking my head, trying to make sense of the conversation. "And who won't let you have your truck? What's going on? What time is it?"

"It's two," he says. "I'm up in Stafford. You know where the courthouse is." He doesn't explain anything else and of course I know better than to push.

"I'll be there in half an hour," I say. I pull on my jeans and grab my wallet and cell phone and tiptoe into Mom's room. The Colonel snores that loud apnea snore of his that is probably the reason Mom always seems so tired during the day. I crouch next to the bed. It's easy to wake her. She opens her eyes and just looks at me for a minute, almost as if she was expecting me.

"It's Jeremy," I say. "I need to borrow the car to go get him."

She glances behind her at the Colonel, and then rolls quietly out of bed.

"What happened this time?" she asks when we're in the kitchen. She fishes through her pocketbook.

"Not sure," I say. "I think he might have gotten arrested. He said something about his truck."

Mom hands me the keys to her car, and a credit card. "Just in case," she says.

Jeremy's truck is sitting in the parking lot outside the sheriff's office at the Stafford Courthouse. He's talking to a deputy when I get there, but he steps away as soon as he sees me. He's in his combat fatigues, what he wears for training.

"Let's go," he says.

44

"Where to?" I ask.

"Back to Quantico," he says, walking past me toward the door. I follow.

I don't get much from him on the fifteen-minute drive. Just that he was on Route 1, driving up to Quantico, when the cops showed up.

"You went home?" I ask. "To see Annie?"

He grunts. "We got in a fight before I left for training. An argument or whatever. I felt bad about it and cut out of work to go talk to her."

"How did that go?" I ask.

"Wonderful," he says. "Like a second fucking honeymoon."

"So why'd you get stopped?"

"Paper bag or some shit blew out in front of me. I swerved and kind of ran a car off the road. Nobody was hurt, just a little shook up. I stopped and checked on them. Would have been a whole lot of nothing but a cop drove by and had me follow him here. I explained. He listened. Said I could get my truck in the morning but that he didn't want me driving tonight. I told him I was fine, but whatever."

I don't smell any liquor on Jeremy, but that doesn't necessarily mean he wasn't drinking.

"You swerved because of a bag?"

"You get trained to do that," he says. "Over there a bag in the road could be an IED."

He pauses, then adds, "Don't say a fucking word about this to Annie. Or anybody."

45

And that's all he says for the rest of the ride. I suspect there's more to the story, but he's not going to tell me any more tonight.

The only good thing about the week is that Jeremy's being gone gives me an excuse to get out of the house and off being grounded. Even the Colonel can't say no to me going over to Annie's after practice to help with the kids and stuff around their house.

The first thing I notice when I get there is an ugly purple bruise on Annie's cheek. "What happened?" I ask.

She lifts her hand to her face, though is careful not to touch it. "It's nothing," she says. "Nelly threw a toy. It happens." And then she changes the subject.

I freeze again a minute later, though, when I see a partial hole in the drywall in the living room. I start to ask her if it was Jeremy, if something happened when he came home last night, but I can't seem to get the words out. It couldn't be him. He would *never* hit Annie, or punch a hole through the wall. He swore practically every day of his life that he'd never be like the Colonel, and told me that I couldn't turn out that way either.

Maybe Annie's not being honest with me about what happened. But whatever caused the hole in the drywall — and the nasty bruise on Annie's face — it couldn't have been Jeremy.

*   *   *

I end up doing all the extra chores over there that the Colonel would have had me doing at home: washing Annie's car, raking the yard again, and bagging the leaves. I spackle over the damaged drywall and touch it up with some leftover paint I find in the garage. I even drag out an extension ladder and clean their gutters. It's still warm enough out, though it's supposed to get cold on the weekend. Nelly cries because I won't let her on the ladder with me, but cheers up when I say maybe I'll take her out for ice cream later, if it's not too late.

"You don't have to do all this," Annie says. She's holding the ladder at the bottom, keeping it steady. Nelly is poking a stick in the black fistfuls of glop I scoop out and toss down on the ground.

"They're really clogged," I say. "You don't want rain spilling over the gutters and down the side of the house. It can get in your windows and stuff."

"That's not what I'm talking about," she says. "All these chores. Taking Nelly for ice cream. You should be off with your friends."

I scoop up more goop and pretend I'm going to throw it on Nelly. She squeals and runs away. The baby's in her playpen, which I set up in the yard. She pulls herself up to standing and watches everything, wide-eyed.

"I'm on restrictions, remember?" I say to Annie. She's still in her nurse's uniform and has her hair pinned up. A single light-brown wisp hangs over one eye, and she keeps brushing it behind her ear with the back of her hand.

"Anyway, I don't mind doing it. It's kind of fun. Really."

Annie rolls her eyes. I wouldn't believe me either. It's actually disgusting work. Fun for Nelly, poking and running, and maybe for Greer, since it's another mysterious thing happening in this strange new world that she's busy trying to figure out, but that's about it. Annie would probably rather be sitting on the couch, putting her feet up after being on them all day at the hospital. I know I'd rather be sitting there with her, listening to her talk about her patients, her coworkers, the asshole doctors.

This girl I went out with for a while, Hannah Marshall, accused me of having a crush on Annie because I spent so much time with her and the kids while Jeremy was deployed. She said it was the way I always talked about Annie, like everything she said was fascinating, and should be as fascinating to Hannah as it was to me. I denied it, of course — the crush on Annie — and told Hannah it was crazy for her to think something like that. But even though I got pissed off, I knew it was probably kind of true. Partly. Not that I'd ever do anything about it, of course. And not that Annie would ever think about me as anything other than just Jeremy's younger brother — too young even to have a full beer all to himself.

Hannah and I eventually stopped going out. Not because I was in love with Annie or anything. I was just busy was all.

* * *

It's getting too dark to do the gutters on the sides of the house, so I put the ladder away. Nelly helps, of course. "Ice cream?" she asks when we're through.

"Not tonight," I say. "I'm pretty sure it's bath time and bedtime. Maybe tomorrow we can go."

Nelly gets her mad look on and crosses her arms. I cave immediately. "You have to go ask your mommy," I say. "It's up to her." I know I shouldn't have said it — that I'm just setting Annie up to be the bad guy — but I've never been very good about saying no to Nelly. Or to Annie, for that matter.

I end up holding Greer while Nelly has an enormous meltdown — kicking at Annie and screaming, splashing water all over the floor when Annie tries to give her a bath. I hear a loud slap, and then silence, and then Nelly starts wailing from what I'm guessing was a quick spanking on her wet bottom.

Annie comes out with Nelly bound up in a big towel, still struggling and wailing. "You should probably go, Shane," she says. "I don't think she's going to calm down for a while."

I tell her I'm happy to stay and take care of Greer while she deals with Nelly. "It's no problem," I say. "I don't have to be anywhere. Just home at some point. But it's no big deal."

I can see Annie weighing her options. On the one hand, she knows I should already be gone. On the other hand, she's a single parent with an overtired kid — one whose tantrum is basically my fault.

So she says, "Just for a little. Just until I can get Nelly

calmed down." She starts to leave the living room for Nelly's bedroom but stops and looks at me.

At some point she put something on her face to cover up the bruise — some sort of makeup, concealer or whatever — but it's still all I can see when I look at her.

"Sometimes I think it's easier when he's not here," she says, Nelly still squirming in her arms. "Even as crazy as it gets." She shakes her head. "I know that's terrible to say."

As if we've been talking about Jeremy all along.

9

I'm the last one to leave practice on Thursday. They give me the wrong play again, and Coach gets pissed off and has me running stadium steps for a whole hour this time, after everybody's gone. There are hardly any cars left in the parking lot when I drag myself out of the shower and head for home. I'm looking around for somebody, anybody, who might give me a ride, because I'm totally leg-dead from all that running, but the only car I recognize is a beat-up old Chevy Nova that belongs to Hannah Marshall. She's not around, though, and even if she were, I figure I'm about the last person she wants bumming a ride, so I keep going. But then I see her, squatting next to her car, fumbling with a jack. That's when I notice the flat.

So I stop. "Hey, Hannah," I say. She's already looking up at me.

"Hey, Shane," she says.

"Got a flat, huh?" I say.

Hannah rolls her eyes. "No," she says, "I just like sitting here. Playing with these neat tools I found in the trunk of my car."

"OK," I say, not exactly surprised by the sarcasm. I probably deserve it for the way I just sort of stopped calling her when we were going out.

"Think you could spare a few minutes?" she asks, nodding at the jack.

I never thought of Hannah as the helpless type. She plays basketball and is almost as tall as I am.

"I've done it before," she says, as if reading my mind. "But the lug nuts are too tight."

She's right. They must have been overtightened with a pneumatic wrench the last time she got new tires or got them rotated or whatever. I have to practically jump up and down on the tire iron to get them loose. Once I do, I slide the jack under, jack the car up, finish taking off the lug nuts and the tire, and pop on her little donut spare.

She thanks me — no sarcasm this time — and we just stand there for a minute, in an awkward silence. She's wearing basketball shorts and a sweaty tank top. Her hair is damp and matted a little on her forehead, but she still looks, well, pretty.

She leaves it to me to break the silence. "So how have you been?" I ask.

"OK," she says. "Busy. What about you?"

"My brother came home," I say. "From overseas."

"Bet that's a big relief," she says. "I saw that YouTube video. Everybody was forwarding it around. Annie must be really happy. And the little girls."

It's funny how she says that, as if she knows them, though she's only ever seen them in passing. I guess because I used to talk about them so much.

For a minute it feels as if Annie is standing right there with us. I'm trying to come up with something else to say, but Hannah saves me from having to.

"I guess I better get going," she says.

"Yeah," I say. And then I say, "Wait. Hannah."

She stops.

"I just wanted to say I'm sorry it didn't work out, us dating and all."

She exhales hard. "Really, Shane?" she says. *"Really?"* But then she shakes it off. "You don't have to apologize. You had a lot going on. It was just bad timing, I guess."

She thanks me again for my help and gets in her car. She doesn't offer me a ride. And the whole way walking home I feel like more of a jerk than before.

* * *

53

Friday night at our game against King George, I get sand-wiched between two of their guys and go down hard on my head. On my helmet, actually, but it doesn't seem to make much difference. My brain hurts so bad I nearly start crying. The trainer has me lie down on a bench while he checks me for signs of concussion, shining a little penlight into my eyes, telling me to follow his finger with my eyes without moving my head, asking me what day it is, who's president. I half-expect him to make me recite the preamble to the god-damn Constitution before he's through.

The thing about Toradol is that even a hit like that you don't feel for too long, even if you are concussed or what-ever. I tell the trainer I'm fine, try to shake off the head thing, and tell Coach I'm ready to go back in the game. He looks at me hard for a second and then orders me to sit tight on the bench, he'll call me when he's good and ready for me to go in. Then he turns his back on me to focus on the game.

This pisses me off and I kick the Gatorade table, sending cups flying and our little student managers scurrying around to pick them all back up and refill them. I slam my helmet down next to me on the bench. My head throbs for a while, and then I just feel kind of dizzy, so that it's difficult to follow the action on the field. Maybe we score. Maybe they score. Maybe nothing happens. I keep thinking I hear somebody calling my name, but when I look around — over at Coach, behind me in the stands, up where Mom and the Colonel always sit, down at the end of the bleachers, where Jeremy sat for part of the game last time — I don't see anyone looking back at me.

So I sit in a kind of a stupor. One of the managers offers me Gatorade, which is very nice of him, considering what I just did to their carefully laid beverage table. Darryl Shook sits down next to me at one point — late in the first quarter? early in the second? — and says, "Serves you right." I can't tell if he's joking around with me and all is forgiven or if he really means it. If so, the dude can sure hold a grudge, I'll give him credit for that.

Coach finally does call my name for real, to go in with the offense, and I jog out on the field, though it's like I'm in a fog, and each footfall rattles my brain. I manage to find the huddle, and know I'm there as a blocking fullback, but I'm not sure I'll be able to focus well enough to remember which blocking scheme to follow when Dee calls the play — even though he's no longer fucking with me now that we're playing an actual game.

I stare up at the blue-black night sky for what feels like the longest time, and then somebody grabs me under my shoulder pads and positions me in the backfield, where I'm supposed to go.

"Thanks," I say. "Sorry."

It's our running back, Adarius Hodges. "Get your head in the game, Dupree," he growls. "Damn, boy."

I nod, and it feels like something's loose in my head, like my brain is floating in sludge.

Dee barks, takes the ball from under center, turns, shoves it into Adarius's gut, and Adarius and I immediately collide into one another, the ball popping out and onto the turf.

Adarius sprawls on the ground — I'm a lot bigger than him, so of course he gets the worst of it — and in a freak bounce, the ball comes right back up into my hands. I don't even have to think about it, I take off running, or take a first step anyway, which is as far as I get before I slam into one of the King George linemen. He seems surprised that I have the ball, or maybe he doesn't quite realize it yet, because he shoves me but doesn't try to tackle me. I get spun around but keep my legs churning and break out of the grasp of another King George lineman — even managing to stiff-arm that guy on the top of his helmet, and down he goes and then I'm free, nothing but open field between me and the goal line.

My head is pounding with every step, but I don't care. I doubt I've ever run this fast. There's a loud roaring in my ears, but also I can distinctly hear the crowd roaring, too, and it makes me happy — them cheering for me, the first time I've gotten to carry the ball all year, thanks to Coach's fucked-up offensive scheme, and here I am, sprinting hard down the middle of the field, only vaguely aware of the fact that there are no King George defenders back here for some reason, and none of our wide receivers down here to block for me either. It's just open field and me sprinting and the ball tucked under my arm and the goal line coming closer even though I can't feel my legs anymore because I'm so deep into oxygen debt.

I hear a thundering sound behind me, and the ragged breath of King George players giving chase, but I'm there now, crossing the goal line, wondering if I should spike the ball or do some sort of NFL dance, only I'm too tired, so I just drop it into the end zone, and when I do, somebody tackles me hard, and I don't even have time to lift my hands to break the fall, I just go down and stay there.

I have no idea how long I lie in the end zone, dirt and grass in my mouth and up my nose and in my eyes. I have no idea how long it takes the referees to clear away the pile on top of me, or how long I'm sitting up with the trainer sticking ammonia under my nose to clear my head, which just won't seem to clear, no matter what, especially when the pain comes back like one of those King George three-hundred-pounders sitting on my head.

They help me up again — second time this game, which is humiliating. I'm usually the one putting the other team's players on the ground so hard that they stay there. I guess it was bound to be my turn someday, karma or whatever, and this is that day.

I'm confused about something, though. As we're walking off, King George's kicker and holder run onto the field. I stop and try to follow where they're going, and sure enough, they're lining up with the rest of the King George team to attempt an extra point.

And then it hits me. Nobody even has to say anything, though I'm sure I'll hear plenty about it later. I got turned around and went the wrong way. I ran the ball into *their* end zone. I scored for them, not us.

The trainer has his hand locked around my arm, guiding me from the field. When we get to the sideline, Coach screams at me. I barely hear him. He grabs my other arm, but I shove past him.

I pull away from the trainer, too, and just keep walking — away from the bench, under the bleachers, and into the locker room. It'll probably get me kicked off the team, but I'm showered and dressed and gone before anybody else shows up.

The game is still going on when I leave — not sure how I'll get home. Mom and the Colonel are probably still up in the stands, wondering what the hell's going on, listening to everybody still laughing their asses off and cursing me for what just happened.

I'm standing alone in the parking lot, my brain still too damn foggy to think straight, when somebody calls my name. I wonder at first if it's the same phenomenon as earlier, when I was sitting on the bench, but then realize there's a familiar truck idling in front of me, twenty feet away. I don't know how long it's been there, and I can't see inside. But I recognize the truck. And the voice.

"Looks like you could stand to escape for a while," Jeremy says. "Hop in and let's get the fuck out of Dodge."

I toss my gym bag in the back and then drag myself in on the passenger side. Jeremy's got a beer between his legs, and he's tucking dip between his lip and gum. Escape. Fuck, yeah. I can't think of anything better than that right at the moment.

"Where we going?" I ask, settling back into the seat, hoping it's a long, long way from here.

"Thought we'd head out to the cabin," Jeremy says, throwing the truck in gear and lurching out of the parking lot. "Got some business to attend to."

I pull a warm beer out of what's left of a twelve-pack on the seat between us and drink half of it without stopping. My head feels like it's about to fall off, but I keep drinking until the can is empty, then slump against the door and press my face to the cool window, which helps a little.

I don't ask what business there is at the cabin — a sort of redneck time-share over near Catlett, where the Colonel has taken us hunting every year since Jeremy was in middle school and I was a little kid. Hard to imagine after all Jeremy's been through in the wars that he wants to go down there and kill some shit.

10

I still have a searing headache when I wake up the next morning on the cabin floor, half in and half out of my sleeping bag. Pressing my hands hard on the sides of my head helps some, but not enough, so I stumble around in search of coffee and aspirin. The only coffee I find is cold — god knows how long ago Jeremy made it; could have been anytime during the night if he didn't sleep, or if he woke up from one of his nightmares. I light the stove and shove the pot on to let it heat up, then find a jumbo bottle of aspirin that probably expired ten years ago. It's sitting next to crusty salt and pepper shakers and a few ancient cans of beans and soup in a rotting cabinet with a door held on by a single rusty hinge. I take four.

Two cups of coffee later the aspirin and caffeine combination kicks in, and my headache mostly lifts, though I still feel like I'm wandering in a thick fog. If I have a concussion, it must not be too bad of one. I go into the bathroom and throw freezing water on my face until the fog starts to clear some, too, and when I come back out, I hear Jeremy outside talking to somebody.

I step over to a dirty window to eavesdrop.

"Every Marine is a rifleman," Jeremy is saying. He's kneeling on the uneven cabin porch with gun parts laid out carefully in front of him on a stained square of canvas. Whoever he's addressing is somewhere off the porch where I can't see.

"The weapon I'm cleaning is the same one every Marine is taught to fire in recruit training. It's the M16-A2. Lightweight, magazine-fed, gas-operated, air-cooled, and shoulder-fired."

He's putting the M16 back together now, not even looking down at the parts, but keeping his eyes fixed on whoever is standing in front of him. While he works he also explains BRASS-F, which he taught me years ago, and which is basically how they teach you to shoot: breathe, relax, adjust, sight, squeeze, fire.

"Now say it back to me," he says. "BRASS-F. What's that stand for?"

I don't hear the answer, but it sounds like a child's

voice responding to Jeremy. I move away from the window and push open the creaky front door, and sure enough, two boys, probably eight and ten years old, are standing there watching Jeremy. I vaguely recognize them as some kids I've seen before who live on a neighboring farm where the Colonel used to stop in on occasion when he brought us here to hunt.

They glance over at me but just for a second, and then back at him.

Jeremy nods to me, his hands still busy reassembling the rifle. He repeats what he said before to the boys: "Breathe, relax, adjust . . ."

Both boys have their hands shoved deep in their jeans pockets. It's cool out. Both have on camouflage hunting jackets and matching caps, too.

Jeremy continues. "The weight of the M16-A2 without sling or magazine is seven-point-seven-eight pounds. Loaded, slung, and ready to fire, it weighs eight-point-seven-nine pounds. It's thirty-nine-point-six-three inches long. Muzzle velocity is thirty-one hundred feet per second."

He pauses, makes some minor adjustments and then keeps going. "The M16 has got a maximum effective range of eight hundred meters on an area target, which is half a mile. On a point target it's five hundred fifty meters. That's about the length of six football fields."

"What's a area target and a point target?" the older boy asks. The other wipes his runny nose on the back of his jacket sleeve.

Jeremy laughs. "What the hell they teaching you monsters in school these days? Point-target range is the distance a trained shooter could hit a target the size of a person. Area-target range is the distance that same shooter could hit some of a group of people."

The younger boy asks Jeremy if he's a trained shooter. Jeremy doesn't laugh this time.

"Yes, I am," he says.

He finishes the reassemblage and slaps a magazine clip into place. There are six more clips on the tarp beside him. He lifts up the M16 to show the boys.

"There are two firing modes for this weapon," he says, his voice the same flat, dry monotone it's been throughout the lecture, or whatever it is. "There's automatic or semi-automatic. On automatic it fires ninety rounds per minute, and on semiauto, forty-five rounds per minute. One of these magazines holds thirty five-point-five-six-millimeter rounds."

"Can we shoot it?" the younger boy asks.

"Yeah, can we?" his brother chimes in.

Jeremy shakes his head. "No. You're not old enough, and you're not Marines."

The younger boy pouts. "Our dad has shotguns. He lets us shoot."

"Good," Jeremy says. "So go ask your dad."

"What you gonna do with that M16?" the older boy asks.

"Kill wild pigs," Jeremy says, shrugging, as if it's obvious.

"Can we come watch?" the older boy asks.

Jeremy shakes his head again. "No. You'll be in bed." He nods over at me. "It'll just be me and him this time."

I can tell by the looks on their faces that the boys have already lost interest in shooting pigs, since they can't come along, but I'm wondering what exactly is involved in this pig-killing project of Jeremy's and how I fit in.

The younger boy asks one last question. "What does something like that cost you?"

Jeremy double-checks the safety and removes the magazine, laying it on the tarp next to the others. "It'll run you about five hundred eighty-six dollars direct from Colt's Manufacturing. If you're a Marine, they give you yours for free. I paid for this one myself anyway."

"You're a Marine, ain't you?" the older boy asks.

Jeremy salutes. "Semper fi, boys."

Later in the morning, Jeremy shows me wild-pig scat and trampled grass, leading up to a peanut field that looks like the aftermath of a Transformers battle. "Wild pigs did this," Jeremy says, somehow the expert on this as he always has been on everything. "They travel in herds and just tear shit up. They can destroy a field like this in a couple of hours. And they don't have any natural predators. I read there are something like three and a half million wild pigs in Texas alone, and they're putting farmers out of business all over the place."

"What about in Virginia?" I ask.

"Not so many," he says. "Just in places like here. But a

sow will produce three litters a year, so they're multiplying like a son of a bitch. And they've gotta eat."

"So let them eat," I say. "What do we care?"

"Can't do it," Jeremy says. "They won't leave anything for deer, turkey, anything else we come here to hunt. They'll chase off all the other wildlife."

I just stand there. I don't really care for hunting, even though the Colonel insisted that we learn to shoot, and bag our quota of turkeys and deer every year — something I never did. It's fine with me if the wild pigs want to take over everything and drive off all the other animals.

"They throw the whole ecosystem out of balance," Jeremy continues. "They destroy all these people's crops around here. But we can help get it back in balance."

"And how are we supposed to do that?"

Jeremy points across the field at a copse of trees, more flattened grass, and a small pond. "Tonight we'll come back. You'll be over there waiting with my 9mm. When they come down to drink, you'll charge out at them and chase them toward me over here."

"What will you do?" I ask, though of course I've already figured out why we're here.

Jeremy pats his M16.

"I'll shoot them when they run."

11

"Do you know what I did last night?" I ask Jeremy. "Did you catch any of the game?"

We're still on the porch outside the cabin. It's just past noon but he's already drinking, sipping from a bottle of Jim Beam. It dawned on me that I have no idea how he happened to show up outside the locker room last night to pick me up from the game.

Jeremy doesn't answer right away, as if it's taking a while for the words to filter through to that part of his brain that makes sense of sound waves: dog barking, jet plane overhead, wind in trees, Shane asking questions.

"Yeah," he says. "I saw it. I showed up right about when it happened. How'd you manage to get so turned around anyway? I've never seen anything quite like it, outside of combat."

"Not sure," I say. "I might have gotten a concussion earlier in the game. Coach had just put me back in. I think something happened to my backup. I was still pretty confused about stuff when we lined up for the play."

Jeremy fiddles with the Jim Beam bottle, lining it up just so on the warped floorboard. We're sitting on the floor, both of us with our legs stretched out, in the early-afternoon sun. There's never been much furniture out here at the cabin. Usually the Colonel or somebody else who has a share in the land will bring old, beat-up lawn furniture, folding chairs, broken-legged card tables, but none of it lasts very long. None of it ever gets carted off either once it breaks down for good. There's a stack of broken crap behind the cabin that's probably home to too many snakes and rats for anybody to do anything about now.

"The way I see it," Jeremy says, "the days of my being the famous one are now officially over. At least as far as being high-school famous. You know, state championship and everything. All that's nothing compared to a guy who runs for a seventy-yard touchdown the wrong way."

I cringe, and decide then and there that I'm never showing my face in the locker room or on the football field again, or anywhere in the vicinity of Coach. Really, I should just insist that Mom and the Colonel let me transfer somewhere. To another town.

"Anyway," Jeremy continues, "when I saw you duck out of the stadium, I figured you needed a mission."

"And what about you?" I ask. "What were you doing there? Why aren't you back at Quantico?"

Jeremy shrugs. "I had to go somewhere and couldn't go home."

I reach for the Jim Beam and have a taste. I've never had hard liquor before. It's awful, burns going down, but I take another drink, which burns even worse than the first one. "They just let you take off?" I ask.

Jeremy draws his legs up out of the sun. It's warm out, and now he's all in shadow.

"Technically you might say I'm UA."

"What's that?"

"Unauthorized Absence," he says.

I sit up straight and turn to face him. "What the hell, Jeremy? I just figured you finished your field training early or something. Now you're telling me you're AWOL?"

"Don't call it AWOL in the Corps," he says, taking the bottle back from me. "I told you. It's UA. Unauthorized Absence. Different thing."

"Quit dicking around," I say, surprised that I'm talking to him this way. He looks surprised, too. If I was one of the men serving under him, I'd probably be in all kinds of trouble.

Jeremy keeps looking at me for a minute, not smiling. Most likely weighing the options for how to deal with a little shithead who thinks he can talk to a Marine captain this way, brother or no brother.

"You done?" he asks evenly.

I duck my head. "Yeah. Sorry." Though I don't exactly know what I'm apologizing for.

Neither one of us speaks for a long time. Neither moves. We just sit there like stones as the afternoon wears on. A fly lands on Jeremy's face and he blows it off. He takes another drink. That's about all. It's a good half hour before he decides to say something else.

"I was supposed to report for a psych eval," he says, his eyes focused on the tree line a hundred yards away, or maybe beyond there, somewhere deeper inside the dark woods. "But I didn't feel like going."

"How come?" I ask softly, my voice even lower than his, barely audible.

"It's complicated," he says.

Three crows set down in the field in front of us, between the cabin and the trees. They don't seem to be eating or looking for food. Just staring at us. Jeremy takes a long drink from the bottle, which is a third of the way gone. The crows step closer to the porch. They're fearless, or stupid. I can't imagine what they think is going to happen. I half expect Jeremy to take up his M16, switch it to automatic, and waste them.

"Complicated how?" I ask after a minute.

He doesn't answer. Just picks up the 9mm, which has been lying on the porch next to him and the M16. Takes lazy aim — definitely not doing the BRASS-F thing. Fires at the crows. Misses. They fly away.

Jeremy doesn't say any more after that. I want to ask him about the psych eval. I want to ask him what happened when he went to see Annie. I want to ask him why she wouldn't talk about it. A part of me wants to yell at him and make him tell me.

But we both know I won't ask him those things. He wouldn't tell me anyway, and just asking would piss him off, and maybe send him running — this time not just away from Annie and the Marine Corps, but away from me, too.

I settle back on the porch and tuck my sweatshirt under my head. I close my eyes and have the feeling that Jeremy's doing the same thing. I hear him breathing, steady. I hear the wind in the trees, whispering softly. Funny how time can stop like that, till you almost believe that nothing will ever change. It'll just be you and your brother, forever, and no more goddamn crows.

12

For the longest time the Colonel wouldn't let me shoot, he just had me sit by him on a deer stand half a mile from the cabin and told me not to complain, no matter how cold it got. That was how one of his foster dads had taught him about the woods and about hunting, he said, but none of it seemed to soak in with me, because all I could ever think about was going home and watching cartoons. It was about the only time the Colonel spent with me or Jeremy, unless he was ragging on us for something, or for nothing, and Mom always got excited when we drove off together to the cabin, as if we would form some sort of magical father-and-son bonds while we were off killing animals.

As bad as the days were, stuck up in the deer stands, the nights were worse. We would wrap ourselves up in all the blankets and sleeping bags we had and try to ignore the cold wind that came in under the door and through the cracks around the windows where the cabin had settled crooked because there was no foundation and the window frames no longer fit right. The Colonel would drink his beer and we'd eat out of cans, and he'd try to teach us stuff about hunting. He might be funny for a little while then, and he might give Jeremy and me a little beer in a cup, but usually he just fell asleep drunk.

The closest I ever came to actually shooting something was lying to the Colonel about shooting something. I must have been about eight or nine years old when it happened. I'd been sitting next to the Colonel on a deer platform for about three hours, since well before the sun came up. Jeremy was in his own stand somewhere else in the woods with his own gun. Either that or he'd already snuck back to the cabin. Anyway, all of a sudden the Colonel got up and said he would be back. He left me with his rifle but told me not to shoot it unless I could absolutely tell it was a buck.

The Colonel hadn't taken a shot all that morning, and I knew he was pissed off about it, but I was pissed off, too, that I couldn't feel my toes and that I could have been home playing football. For no good reason I took a shot at a tree not too long after he left. The Colonel came running back, excited that I might have killed something, though I could tell that he was also kind of pissed at the thought that I'd gotten a shot when he hadn't. But of course there was nothing, and I said I must have missed. He scowled at me and said, "Come on," and pretty soon we were walking on the dirt road under the power lines, him with the gun, me with the knapsack, which held the sandwiches we'd packed for lunch and all the crushed cans from the beer the Colonel had been drinking that morning. Then, right there in the middle of the road in front of us, was a doe and her fawn.

The doe started, ears up, eyes wide, and bolted into the trees. But the fawn didn't follow.

"Why didn't you shoot that deer?" I asked the Colonel, and he said it was like he already told me, you couldn't shoot a doe right then, and you'd lose your hunting license if you did and got caught.

Neither one of us took our eyes off the fawn. I kept expecting him to bolt into the trees with his mom, but he didn't. Instead he lowered his head and walked right toward us, kind of quickly, too. He veered toward the Colonel, who took too long to step out of the way, and the fawn butted him in the thigh. The Colonel did a kind of dance to try to get away, but the fawn kept butting him with his little head, back and back up the road, the Colonel doing his crazy dance the whole time. I laughed so hard I rolled in the road on top of the sandwiches.

That was the only time I can remember ever coming close to liking him.

*   *   *

I'm crouching behind a fat water oak, downwind from the creek where Jeremy is sure the wild pigs will come to drink. It's dusk, but the deepening shadows in the woods don't let in much light from the fading sun. I feel for the holster on my hip and pull out the 9mm. It feels slick and oily and fits perfectly into my hand.

I don't plan to shoot at any of the pigs, just fire into the air. But who knows if it'll even come to that. Just because we found their trails leading this way, that doesn't mean they'll show. They must have access to water all over the place.

I'm worried about Jeremy, up that hill somewhere, also hiding. He's got the M16 and all those ammunition clips. The Jim Beam is half gone, and he's all the way drunk. I had to practically carry him here from the cabin, and then prop him up against the trunk of a fallen tree. But he waved me on in the direction of the creek, and so I went.

Maybe I should have tried to talk him out of this. I know it's dangerous. But my whole life I've always just gone along with whatever Jeremy wanted, no questions asked. I just went for it. Jumping off high bridges into rivers. Crawling through dark, nasty culverts under highways. Swiping candy bars from convenience stores.

I knew Jeremy was proud of me back then, even if he never said so. He always shared the money with me if I did stuff like crawl in an open sewer so he could win a bet with his friends. I'd do just about anything he said. Plus he was always so funny back then, no matter how bad things were at home with the Colonel. One time when we were both really pissed off at the Colonel, Jeremy got a razor blade and very carefully cut most of the stitching out of the butt seams in the Colonel's pants, and for weeks there was an epidemic of pants splitting every time the Colonel bent over. He kept asking Mom if she thought he'd put on weight lately. From the way she fought to keep from smiling, or laughing, I wondered if she suspected Jeremy was somehow to blame. I thought it was the funniest thing ever.

So it isn't in my genetic makeup or whatever to say no to Jeremy, to tell him he's too drunk to be holding an M16, too wasted to be hunting wild pigs out here in the middle of nowhere in the dark.

I hear them before I see them, snuffling through the tall grass and down to the water, just like Jeremy said they'd do. At first they're just dark shapes, snorting and splashing and grunting, a lot more of them than I expected. Dozens, maybe. Maybe more.

They're not like any pigs I've ever seen before at farms. As they gradually come into focus, I can make out their black, bristly coats, narrow snouts, and, on some of the bigger ones, long tusks. A couple are enormous. They could pass for small hippos. I can't believe how loud they are, jostling for space at the water's edge, or splashing all the way in. I grip the 9mm tighter, suddenly nervous about running out and surprising them. I consider just staying right where

I am, frozen behind my tree. Maybe the pigs will wander off and Jeremy will never know they were here. Maybe he's passed out and won't know even if I *do* send them his way.

But what if he's not? What if he's heard them, too, and is waiting, his M16 locked and loaded?

I push myself up to standing, take the safety off the pistol, swallow hard, and then charge out from behind the tree, yelling and firing — not into the air for some reason, but toward the water's edge. The pigs start squealing and running — wounded, panicked, who knows — tearing up the hill toward Jeremy. I keep yelling and charging and shooting, not sure how many shots, till they're gone. All except one, which lies on its side in the water.

I leave it there and follow the herd, but before I make it clear of the trees, Jeremy opens fire. He's got the M16 on automatic, which must mean he's not even bothering to aim.

I press my hands over my ears to block out the sounds of the slaughter.

13

I can't tell how many clips Jeremy empties into the wild pigs, but the shooting and the squealing seem to go on forever. At one point I realize that Jeremy is yelling, too, though not anything intelligible, just this raw, hoarse shout mixed with the blasting of the M16 and the suffering sounds of the pigs.

And then it stops — the shooting, the yelling. Everything except the wild, plaintive squealing of wounded pigs. I make my way up the hill, surprised that the moon is so bright. Jeremy is sitting on the fallen tree, his rifle leaning next to him. And scattered all around the field are the bodies. I walk through them and can't not see heads exploded, legs shot off, sides split apart, entrails spilling out on the ground, blood pooling everywhere.

Jeremy calls over to me. "Come here, Shane." His voice sounds odd, faint somehow.

"No!" I yell back. I don't want to be anywhere near him. I want to run away from this place, from all this blood.

"Goddamnit, come here!" Jeremy shouts, though there's not much weight to how he says it.

I go over anyway. "What?"

"Take the rifle," he says. "I need you to finish them off."

"No way," I say. "*You* did this. You started it, so you finish it." I don't tell him that I already killed one, back at the river.

"Take the goddamn rifle," he says through gritted teeth. "It's on single shot. Or use the 9mm. Either way. Put one through the back of their head, at the base of the skull."

"Why don't you do it?" I ask sullenly.

"Because one of the little fuckers gored me with his tusk," he says, and he lifts one of his hands. There's blood on it. He keeps his other hand clamped hard over his right thigh, up near his groin.

He picks up the M16 with the bloody hand. "Charged right at me while I was shooting."

"How bad is it?" I ask.

"How the hell should I know?" he says. "I don't think he hit the femoral artery, if that's what you're asking. But he got me pretty good."

"We've got to get you to the hospital," I say.

He shoves the M16 into my chest. "Finish the job. Then we'll see."

I know there's no arguing with him. Once he has his mind set on something, there's no changing it with Jeremy.

I grab the M16, though I'm not entirely sure I know how to use it.

"I already loaded a new ammunition clip," he says. "So get going."

I walk hesitantly off to where the pigs are and find one that's still alive. It isn't making any noise, but its eyes are open and it's sort of shuddering. Half of it is gone. I aim where Jeremy told me to, but I can't squeeze the trigger.

This is crazy. I'd be putting it out of its misery, I know that. Only I can't do it. Everything about this just feels wrong.

I go back to Jeremy, not saying anything.

He spits on the ground in disgust. "Jesus Christ. Just give me the weapon."

He limps out into the field, one hand still holding his thigh, so he's hunched over. Then he finishes off the pigs. He doesn't even hesitate. He just does it. Five of them. Six. And then he finds a couple of piglets, rooting at a female's udders. They're not hurt at all, as far as I can tell, though I'm not all that close. Jeremy shoots them, too.

Everything's quiet now. The ones that escaped the shooting are long gone, probably off eating up somebody else's field. Jeremy hobbles back over and slumps onto the ground.

"Take off your shirt," he says. "Tie it tight around my leg here. Then go get the truck."

I'm wearing a flannel shirt over a T-shirt and take off both.

Jeremy leans his head back against the fallen tree. I tie the T-shirt on for the tourniquet, then grab my flannel shirt and race off into the dark.

There are no doctors in or near Catlett, as it turns out, but I manage to find a veterinarian who agrees to take a look at Jeremy. "I generally work out in the barn there," the vet says. "But I guess inside's OK." I'm half carrying Jeremy and we're standing on the vet's front porch.

He lays a tarp down on the living room floor, and I deposit Jeremy there. The vet's wife comes in with a pillow and tucks it under Jeremy's head. The vet pokes and prods, pours some sort of antiseptic over the wound, packs gauze around it, then bandages Jeremy up.

"No damage to the femoral artery," he says. "You were darn lucky there. Those tuskers can do some serious hurt when they attack. Had a hunting dog in here, whole entire throat was about gone from him mixing it up with a wild boar."

He shakes his head, remembering. "Anyway, I'd say we ought to get you on up to the hospital. Only so much I can do here."

"What hospital?" Jeremy asks.

"Manassas," the vet says. "Half hour, forty-five minutes at the most. Doubt you'll be too comfortable laid out in the back of your truck that whole way, though. Best let me make a call."

Jeremy doesn't say anything else, and the vet takes that for an OK.

Ten minutes later, an old guy shows up, driving a hearse. He's wearing pajamas.

"You're kidding me, right?" Jeremy says.

"Best we can do," the vet says. Apparently there's no ambulance in the whole little town either.

I thank him and pull some money out of Jeremy's wallet. He waves me off. "You boys just take care," he says. And then, looking at Jeremy, he says, "We thank you for your service."

Jeremy nods and shakes his hand.

"You ever been in one of these before?" the man from the funeral home asks as we load Jeremy in the hearse.

"Drove something like it once," Jeremy says. "Over in Afghanistan."

The man nods as if he understands on some deeper level.

I drive Jeremy's truck behind the hearse down a dark, empty highway to Manassas. Trees crowd the road so close that it seems like you'd hit one head-on if you so much as drifted onto the shoulder.

I pick up my cell phone. I've been avoiding it all day. There are about twenty texts and a bunch of voice mails, but I don't read or listen to any of them. I already know what they say. The Colonel is probably so pissed off that I'll never be able to go home again. Coach has probably kicked me off the team. Mom's probably called every law enforcement agency in Virginia. God knows what sort of search they have on for Jeremy.

I call Annie. It's late, pushing midnight, but she answers right away.

"Shane, where are you?" she asks before I say anything. "Your parents are worried sick. Everybody's worried. Are you all right?"

"I'm OK," I say. "Sorry. I'm just up at the cabin. With Jeremy."

Annie doesn't speak for a minute, like she's too afraid to ask.

"He's all right," I say. "He got stuck in the leg by a wild boar, but it's not too bad. We saw somebody already, but they're sending us up to Manassas to get it checked out. It's nothing serious. Really."

"Wild boar? He's supposed to be at work."

"I know," I say, my eyes fixed on the red taillights of the hearse in front of me. "He told me. Did somebody call there?"

"Yes, of course they called," she says, angry. "What did he think they would do? It's the Marines, not some stupid job at Walmart."

"I know," I say again.

"Let me speak to him," she says. The baby's crying in the background and Annie practically has to shout.

"He can't talk right now," I say. "He's . . . he's sleeping. But I'll tell him to call you after we get there, after he gets looked at. Anyway, I'm sure he'll be able to straighten everything out. With the Marines and whatever." I'm practically stuttering, and wanting to get off the phone without having to tell Annie anything else. "Can you call my mom?" I ask her. "Just let her know what's going on and where I am and all. I'll be home tomorrow."

"Tell her what's going on?" Annie repeats. "You still haven't told *me* what's going on."

But I don't know what to say. So there's just a long silence over the phone between us. Greer's crying gets louder, and now I hear Nelly, too. I wonder if whoever called from Quantico told her about the psych eval they ordered for Jeremy, but from the way she's talking I doubt it.

"I have to go," Annie says, all the anger drained out of her voice, replaced by what sounds like exhaustion.

"Make him get help," she whispers before hanging up. "And don't let him take you down, too."

They give Jeremy painkillers at the hospital — I guess he's sobered up enough — and then make me leave the room while they scrub out the wound again. "He's not going to like this," a nurse tells me.

"His wife is a nurse," I tell her, as if she might need the information.

She just looks at me blankly.

I pace around the waiting room, mostly oblivious to the others in there, too worked up to be tired, replaying the conversation with Annie. Talking to her has brought me back to reality, or something like it — worrying about what's going to happen when I go back home and have to face up to everything that's happened.

My cell phone digs into my thigh, and I pull it out to check all those messages I've been ignoring. Four are from Mom. A couple of guys on the team texted. "WTF, Shane? At least we still won."

Annie left two voice mails, several hours ago. "Shane, sweetie, I don't know what's going on, but you have to call, OK? Call soon."

Hannah Marshall also texted, which surprises me. She sent it last night after the game. Kind of strange, I guess, but it makes me happy to see her name come up.

"Hey. Saw what happened. Hope you're all right. I did the same thing once in a basketball game. Got turned around and scored for the other team. I survived. Thanks again for helping with the flat."

I save the text.

They're planning to keep Jeremy overnight so they can test for nerve damage in the morning, but he's got other ideas.

"Let's go," he says, right after they bring him his clothes. He's in a double room with a guy who already looks dead — a coma victim who seems to be barely breathing. I wonder why he's not in intensive care. A note on a whiteboard next to his bed says "Call home."

I help Jeremy into his fatigues, which are hard to put on

because they're so stiff from dried blood. He's woozy from the painkillers, so I swipe a wheelchair from out in the hall and off we go.

"What's the big rush?" I ask, thinking I don't want to go home, now or ever.

"I hate hospitals," Jeremy says. "That's one."

"What's two?" I ask as the front doors open automatically to let us out into the night. It's gotten colder out.

"Pigs," he says. "Can't leave them in the field. They'll rot and stink and it'll piss off the guy that owns the cabin. We'd never hear the end of it from the Colonel."

"So what do we do with them?"

"Don't know," Jeremy says. "Need to think about it on the way back." We're at the truck now, where I left it in the ER parking lot. I help him up on the passenger side, annoyed that he's only now trying to come up with a plan. Jeremy's the guy who has a plan for everything, even if we don't always follow it. A plan for running away from the Colonel when we were little. A plan for rescuing Mom.

I want him to have a plan for how I'm ever going to go back to school and face the football team. I want him to have a plan for himself — not for just getting his psych eval and finding out what's wrong with him, but for getting well, too.

Jeremy has me stop at the cabin, though we're inside for less than a minute. The first light of dawn is sneaking in through the trees like it's going to steal something. I'm so tired I could throw up.

"C'mon," Jeremy says, limping back to the truck. "Don't even think about sitting down."

He takes a swig from the bottle of Jim Beam. I realize this is the only reason he had me stop at the cabin. "You shouldn't be drinking that," I say. "Jesus, Jeremy. You're on drugs."

He takes another swig, then caps the bottle and tosses it to me. "You want some, all you have to do is say."

I drag myself back up into the truck and we bounce down a rutted track from the cabin out into the fields.

"Stop here," Jeremy says after a few minutes. "This is the place."

I don't recognize anything, and start to say it — that he's wrong, that he's too messed up on the painkillers and the booze to figure out where we need to go. But then I see a couple of gray mounds twenty yards in front of us.

"So what do we do with them?" I ask. "Can we burn them? Make a big pile?"

Jeremy shakes his head, pulling on the door handle and easing himself onto the ground. "No water. Fire could spread. We could burn down the whole field. The whole forest."

"There's water down the hill," I point out. "Where the pigs came down to drink. Remember?"

"And you think you can get that water *up* the hill how, exactly?" Jeremy asks, his voice heavy with slurred sarcasm.

"Fine," I say. "Then, what?"

He spits. "Throw them in the back of the truck. We'll have to take them somewhere."

"Are you fucking crazy?" I snap. "There's no way. Those aren't even pigs. They're pieces of pigs. And where are you — are *we* — going to take them?"

Jeremy grabs the front of my jacket and jerks me close to him, his face inches from mine. I'm taller than him and outweigh him by probably thirty pounds, but it doesn't feel that way. I flinch.

He lets go and I stagger backward a couple of steps. He looks up at the soft-blue sky for a long time. Then, oddly, he starts whistling. I don't recognize the song.

"Back up the truck to those first ones over there." He points to the two gray mounds I saw before. "We'll start with them."

We don't have a liner to protect the truck bed. We don't have gloves. We don't have anything. Just our hands and our backs. We work in silence, lifting bodies, legs, half-severed heads, entrails, other remains. I gag repeatedly. The only reason I don't vomit is because I haven't eaten in nearly two days.

Jeremy whistles again—not a song—as he holds up separate halves of a small pig that's been blown completely apart. "M16 can flat do some damage," he says, shaking his head. Tracks of sweat are streaking down his face. At least I think it's sweat.

I shut down my mind as best I can and keep loading up the truck until we're through. It's not possible to count how many pigs Jeremy slaughtered, the carcasses are such a mess. We're both covered in pig blood long before we're through. I'll never wear these boots again, I know that much. Or these jeans, or this jacket or shirt.

The sun's visible over the trees by the time we finish. I sit on the ground and lean against the truck. Jeremy eases himself down next to me. I'm thinking about that one last pig down the hill, the one I shot last night in the water. Wondering if I should tell Jeremy, if we should get that one, too, or if I can just say nothing and leave it.

The kids from the day before materialize out of the woods and are standing right in front of us before it fully registers that they're here.

They stare and we stare, too tired to speak. I don't know how Jeremy is still conscious. I'm not sure how I am either, but at least I'm not on painkillers, and I don't have a hole in my leg. I wonder if he's bleeding through the gauze and bandages, but with all the pig blood on us, there's no way to tell.

"What y'all doing with those pigs?" the older boy finally asks. His little brother picks his nose until the older boy swats at his hand to make him stop.

"Taking them to the pig cemetery," Jeremy says.

The older boy crosses his arms. "There's no such thing as a pig cemetery."

"Yeah," says the nose picker. "Y'all are stealing them."

Jeremy looks at his bloody hands and then back up at the boys. "Can't steal wild pigs," he says. "Tell your daddy we did him a favor. They were tearing up your fields."

"Still some out there," the older boy says. "Got in the vegetable garden next to the house last night. You probably scared them, so they went over there when you shot these ones."

Jeremy wipes his hands in the grass. Some of the blood comes off, but not much. "Can't kill them all," he says.

"We're telling our daddy," the little boy says.

Jeremy shrugs and turns to me. "Let's get out of here. Maybe we can run over these little dudes on the way out."

The boys don't stick around after that. "Come on, Dickie," the older boy says, grabbing his brother's arm. They take off running back through the field, disappearing into the woods that produced them in the first place.

We drive back into Catlett and ask around. Somebody directs us to a feed store, and a guy there says we might drive over the mountains to Woodstock, Virginia. "That's the closest rendering plant," he says. The way he says it, you'd think people are driving around town all the time with a truck bed full of dead pigs, rotting and stinking in the morning sun.

When we hobble back outside to the truck, a middle-aged woman in a hunting jacket and wading boots is standing next to it, looking over the carcasses.

"How much you take for these?" she asks, in a voice you might expect to hear from a Sunday school teacher. She has a Sunday school teacher's face, too — soft, even kind. But she seems to be all business. "I'll pay good money."

"Not for sale," Jeremy says, and that's the end of the conversation.

I can't begin to imagine what the woman would want with the pigs, but neither of us asks. I'm not sure I want to know.

I feel like I've left the real world so far behind that we might never make it back.

"What's a rendering plant?" I ask Jeremy once we're

back on the road, heading west now over the Shenandoah Mountains.

"It's where they boil down dead animals, or the remains of them," he says.

"What for?"

"Lots of things."

"Like what?"

"Feed it to other pigs."

16

"Do you think they're looking for you?" I ask Jeremy. "The military police?"

We're still in the truck, climbing switchbacks up the mountains. I'm glad to be driving so I don't get carsick, but I have to keep slapping myself to stay awake. Maybe a conversation with Jeremy will help.

"Go faster," is all he says at first. "Every time you slow down, the stink from those pigs catches up to us."

I press the accelerator harder and steel myself as we approach the next curve. It feels like my hanging on tight to the steering wheel is all that keeps us from flying off the road and crashing down the side of the mountain.

Jeremy takes out a pocketknife and busies himself digging dried blood and dirt out from under his fingernails. We're both still covered in pig blood, though we washed with soap and scrubbed as hard as we could when we stopped for gas.

"Doubt it," he says, long after I've given up the thread of the conversation. It takes me a minute to remember what we were talking about.

Then he says, "They wouldn't be in any big rush to throw an Article Eighty-six at me. They probably just called the house. I've got a couple of messages on my phone." He slides it out of his pocket and stares at the black screen for a minute. Then, as casually as if it's an apple core, Jeremy rolls down the window and tosses his cell phone down the side of the mountain.

I hit the brakes. "What the hell, Jeremy! What did you do that for?"

"Keep driving," he growls. "I told you. Fucking stinks in here when you slow down."

I yank the truck back on the road and keep going. Jeremy rolls up his window and stares straight ahead up the highway.

"What are we going to do after we get rid of these pigs?" I ask. I wish I'd thought to get some water when we stopped for gas. I'm desperately thirsty, and my tongue feels swollen, so it sounds funny when I speak.

I know we should head straight home, of course. But I have a feeling Jeremy's no more eager than I am to face the shitstorms waiting there for both of us. A lot less eager, probably.

"We should probably get something to eat," he says. "And something else to drink." He unscrews the top on the Beam and takes a long drink. It makes him shudder, but he takes another and then hands it to me.

"No, thanks," I say, but he won't take it back so I have a sip. It burns the same way it did the first time I tried it.

Jeremy leans back and pulls his baseball cap low over his face, and I'm all alone, riding the brakes down the far side of the mountain until I can smell them burning. I ease off, and the next thing I know, I'm going too fast to control the truck, so I'm alternately downshifting and riding the brakes the whole rest of the way down.

We're twenty miles from Woodstock when I pull over, figuring I should let the brake pads cool off before they catch fire or something, and also so I can close my tired eyes and take a nap and maybe not drive off the side of the road, which has been threatening to happen for the past half hour.

It's one of those crappy picnic areas they put beside the highway for no apparent reason. No restrooms, no scenic views, no grills, no lake or river or pond, no playground equipment. Just a couple of weather-worn picnic tables and a couple of forty-gallon drums filled with trash, with heavy metal lids and concrete blocks on top so raccoons can't get in.

I park as far off the road as I can. Jeremy's totally crashed and doesn't wake up, and pretty soon — about as long as it takes me to turn off the engine — I'm dead asleep, too, and dreaming I'm with Annie and the kids. We're running. Not from anything, exactly, and not toward anything. Just running. Annie and I keep having to slow down. She's carrying Greer and I've got Nelly's hand, but they keep dropping stuff and we have to pick it up. There's too much stuff — toys and dolls and bottles and diaper bags — and I tell Annie we should just get rid of it, just toss it, or leave it, but she says, "No, no, we can't. We have to hold on to everything."

I wake up with a start, not knowing where I am or how long I've been asleep. It's stifling in the cab, and I immediately gag from the overpowering stench from the dead pigs in the back. I fling open the door and stagger away from the truck until I can breathe again, and then look back. A swarm of black flies has descended on the carcasses, and it's got to be the most disgusting thing I've ever seen.

Holding my breath, I run back over to the truck, thinking I should wake Jeremy up and drag him out before he gets asphyxiated.

I open the door and shake him. "Jeremy!"

The next thing I know, I'm on the ground and he's on top of me, yelling, his hands around my throat, squeezing. I can't speak, can't make a sound. I'm just flailing and gasping and his face above mine is purple with rage. He's blind to me, blind to everything, and choking me and choking me until things get fuzzy at the edges of my vision and I'm sure I'll pass out. In some desperate reflex I hammer my forearms up hard against his, just hard enough to loosen his grip on my throat so I can roll out from under him, but he's still in that blind rage and comes after me. I swing my fist and catch him above the ear, which slows him down but doesn't stop him, so I hit him again, but then he's on top of me again and he has his knife out and I'm screaming his name: "Jeremy! Don't! *Jeremy!*"

And he stops. He rolls off me and I go limp. He sits in the dirt next to me and looks at the knife. There's blood on the blade, and I realize he must have cut me. I put my hand to my cheek and feel it.

I lift up on my elbows and scoot away in case he freaks out again. I don't stop until there's a good ten feet of parking lot between us. Jeremy wipes the knife blade off on his fatigues, closes it, and slips it back in his pocket.

We smell the rendering plant a couple of miles before we get there — hot vomit and garbage, rotting and burning flesh, burnt copper. The building is long and low, with five tall gray vats behind it, and several pens holding the sickliest animals I've ever seen: Horses so emaciated I can count every rib. Cows lying on their sides, big tongues lolling out of half-open mouths in the dirt. Goats and sheep, their breathing ragged, their eyes desperately wide.

Our dead wild pigs will be right at home.

I'm about ready to start dry heaving just sitting here in the parking lot; if there's a hell, this has to be how it smells. But Jeremy is in no apparent hurry to get out of the truck.

"Don't ever do that again — wake me up like that," he says out of nowhere. "You're damn lucky I didn't hurt you."

I resist the urge to rub my bruised neck, or finger the crusted-over cut on my cheek. "Sorry," I mumble.

Jeremy never could — or would — apologize for anything. I always ended up being the one to smooth things over by saying sorry and taking the blame.

Except when it came to the Colonel. Jeremy wouldn't ever let the Colonel punish me for anything if he could help it. If I broke a lamp or stole cookies, Jeremy took the blame — and the Colonel's punishment, which was a belt whipping, or a hard shove across the room, or knuckles on the back of his head. Once when I accidentally knocked a mirror off the wall and it shattered into a million pieces, the Colonel got so mad that he slammed Jeremy's head into a door.

Too late I started screaming, "Jeremy didn't do it! It was me! It was me!"

Jeremy went for his baseball bat and told the Colonel that if he ever touched him again — or so much as thought about hurting me or Mom — Jeremy would kill him.

Jeremy lied to Mom about the hole in the door. He said we'd been playing football in the house. Mom just stood there, staring at the hole, even though she must have guessed the truth.

But nobody talked about stuff like that in our family. Not the Colonel. Not Jeremy. Not Mom. Not even me.

*   *   *

A short guy in an oversize security guard uniform comes to the office door, or what we guess is the office. It isn't marked. He looks younger than me, with one of those cherub faces, but has a large gun in a black holster on his hip, and a large wad of tobacco stuffed inside one cheek. He looks at us, blinks, and spits a stream of black juice that lands too close to Jeremy's boot. Not a good start.

"What you want?" he asks in a deep country accent. The name sewn over his big shirt pocket says "Nutt."

"Are you Mr. Nutt?" Jeremy asks.

The guard looks down at his shirt as if to check and then nods.

"Well, Mr. Nutt," Jeremy says, "we have some pigs for your rendering plant. Where do you want them?"

Nutt spits again. "They're closed."

Jeremy shifts his weight away from his injured leg. "What do you mean 'closed'? We're just dropping off. We'll unload them ourselves. So just point us to where."

"Can't do it," says Nutt. He looks us up and down more closely, taking in our blood-covered clothes, and dirt-smeared faces from the parking-lot fight. Jeremy has some swelling around his eye where I hit him. God knows what I must look like.

"Tell you what, Mr. Nutt," Jeremy says. "Either you direct us to where we should deposit these fine specimens we have in our truck, or we'll dump them right here in your little parking lot and you can clean up the mess."

Nutt takes a step backward toward the office door. He

suddenly looks even younger — and scared. "You better not," he says, putting his hand on the handle of his gun.

Something's about to happen — I can feel it coming off Jeremy in waves — so I step in front of him, fishing in my pocket for whatever money I have.

"Here you go," I say, shoving some bills toward Nutt — a ten and a five and a couple of ones. "Maybe this can help. OK? What do you think? Just a little something to help you out here."

He hesitates. Glances over my shoulder at Jeremy, looks back at me, then takes the money.

"Deadstock goes around back," he says. "I guess I can go unlock the gate. There's a raw-material bin right there by the loading dock. Next to the hogger shredder. You can back your truck in. I ain't touching those pigs, though." He looks at the bills I just gave him. "Not for any money."

"No problem," I say quickly, not wanting Jeremy back in the conversation.

It takes us an hour to unload all the pigs, which have decayed a lot since last night. I find a rag in the truck and tie it around my face to block the stench. Jeremy doesn't bother. He flinches every now and then when something bangs into his leg, but you wouldn't know he was hurt otherwise.

Then he goes over to an outside faucet, turns it on, uncoils a long hose, and drags it back over to the truck. It takes fifteen minutes to wash out all the blood and entrails.

Nutt's curiosity finally gets the better of him. "How'd y'all kill these anyway?" he asks.

".22," Jeremy says, lying.

"No way," Nutt says. ".22 don't do damage like that."

"M16," I say, and Nutt nods.

"Knew it," he says. "So how come y'all didn't turn them boys in for the bounty?"

"There's a bounty?" I ask. I look at Jeremy to see if he's heard, but he's looking down at the pile of pigs and their limbs and guts and severed heads — all that carnage now swimming in a soup of their own blood.

He doesn't look sad, exactly, but something not that far from it. Whether it's about the pigs or the bounty or something else altogether, I'll probably never know.

18

It's late Sunday afternoon, nearly dusk, and we've only been gone since Friday night, but it feels as if Jeremy and I are in a different country, and we've been here for so long I almost can't remember how to get back home. A part of me wants to be there right now, showered and clean and crawling into bed to sleep until school on Monday. But another part of me knows that Jeremy isn't ready to go home, and I can't leave him.

Just outside of town, we come upon a sign for River Riders, one of those outdoor adventure places. Jeremy points. "Pull over there."

"You want to go rafting?" I ask, wondering if he's joking.

He shrugs. "You got any better ideas?"

The turnoff is just a mile farther and I take it, slowing considerably as we ease down a steep gravel road that takes us to the North Fork of the Shenandoah River. Minutes later we pull up to a log building surrounded by canoes and kayaks and piles of black inner tubes and large yellow rafts. Orange life vests hang over a long clothesline between two massive fir trees. There's a blue-painted school bus parked in the lot, with the words "River Riders" on the side, and a loaded canoe trailer on the back, also painted blue.

"Now what?" I ask.

Jeremy opens his door. "Now we go rent ourselves a canoe."

"You're kidding?" I say. But he hops down from the truck and closes the door.

"We can't go in there," I say, following him. "Look at us. They'll think we just murdered somebody."

Jeremy shrugs. "I'll explain."

"Explain what?" I ask. "Anyway, I have to get back. I have school tomorrow. Mom's already worried sick. And you should get home to Annie and the kids. She needs to know that you're OK."

"Already texted her," he says, which I know is a lie.

"Well, I have to get back," I say again. "And I'm tired and it's getting late, and these guys probably aren't even open."

Jeremy pulls his wallet out of his pocket and extracts a credit card, waving it at me. "Oh, they'll be open."

Minutes later we're standing inside the River Riders' store, picking out clothes and supplies. They have plenty of both, as it turns out. A Grizzly Adams type in a flannel shirt, working the counter, asks Jeremy about all the blood in a matter-of-fact way, and Jeremy explains about the wild pigs and the rendering plant, leaving out the part about the M16 and getting gored.

"From the looks of you boys, there must be quite a few less of those pigs than there was," he adds politely. Then he asks if we want to use their outdoor shower.

"Appreciate that," Jeremy says, as we bag up all our food and gear: two sleeping bags, a small stove, a cook kit, a river guide, and a couple of self-inflating mattresses.

"Can't let you have the canoe until the morning," the guy says, half apologizing. "But I'll go ahead and bring it over to the landing so you can take off first thing in the morning if you want. And there's room under the picnic shelter next to the river for y'all to lay out your sleeping bags."

The showers have cold water only and I'm freezing the whole time I'm under, scrubbing hard with a rough bar of soap to get off all the blood. It's gotten dark out, but the store's back-porch light is still on. The North Fork flows black and quiet not far off. Jeremy's standing next to me, also stripped down naked. He's fit and lean, but too thin, his ribs showing kind of like those poor horses' back at the rendering plant.

We step out of the showers at the same time, drying off with towels the guy threw in on top of the gear we bought.

Jeremy peels the dressing from his thigh wound and cleans off the blood with an antiseptic wipe, then presses clean gauze pads back over it and tapes the gauze to his leg.

The new clothes fit OK — a bunch of North Face stuff. God knows how much Jeremy charged on his credit card. I don't think he even looked at prices, or at the bill.

"I'll be right back," he says, and he hikes up the hill and around the store to the parking lot. I stay back to stack everything we just bought on the picnic tables under the shelter. With the showers turned off I can hear the river more clearly now, a soft, low murmuring, with a distant grumbling from small rapids, if you can even call them that, on the other side, and I want nothing more right now than to crawl into my sleeping bag and fall asleep to the sounds of it.

Jeremy has other ideas. He's back a few minutes later with the M16, a tarp, and some other things from the truck — including the bottle of Jim Beam, though there's not much left. Just a couple of fingers' worth in the bottom.

"Let's go," he says.

"Now?" I say. "But the guy said he doesn't want us taking the canoe out until morning."

Jeremy grabs one of the bags of new gear. "I just talked to him. It's OK. We'll camp down the river a ways."

I don't bother to argue that it's too dark, too late, not safe — all the reasonable things. I don't say that I don't believe Jeremy talked to the guy again either. I just pick up the sleeping bags and whatever else I can carry, and pretty soon we've packed everything into the canoe the guy hauled out for us earlier.

We slide the canoe over to the landing and halfway into the water. I climb in front. Jeremy hands me a paddle. He climbs in back, pushes us off into the river, and steers us into the middle, where we catch the current. Minutes later the lights from the River Riders store disappear as we glide around the bend and out of sight to the rest of the world.

I dip my paddle into the blue-black water and pull, half a dozen strokes on one side, half a dozen on the other, and then the exhaustion hits, like being sandwiched all over again by those two King George linemen. I lay the paddle across the bow and lean forward against it, letting my head rest on my arms. Everything hurts, and this bone-deep fatigue leaves me too tired to even speak, to ask Jeremy — or beg him — please, can't we just pull over to the bank and sleep?

He's not paddling either, just steering, keeping us in the slow-moving current. The river's doing all the work. It's getting darker by the minute, though there's enough moon to cast long shadows and create diamonds on the water where waves catch the light. I lift my head and see owls on the riverbank and bats darting past the canoe. Something screeches. Something splashes. Something growls. The sounds carry so well here that it's impossible to know where anything starts.

I lean back and settle on the mound of gear in the middle of the boat. It's chilly on the river, so I zip up my North Face jacket and pull a knit cap down over my ears, then close my eyes, serenaded by the soft rocking of the canoe and the hush of the water as we glide farther downstream.

I wake up what must be hours later, under a sleeping bag in the canoe, which has been pulled up on a flat, sandy place on the riverbank. The half-moon is high overhead, blotting out the stars. I shift to make myself comfortable on the hard, lumpy gear I've been lying on, finally find a position where nothing's digging into my back, and then sit up suddenly.

Where's Jeremy?

He's not in the canoe. Not anywhere nearby on this little spit of beach. I struggle to push myself up and climb out of the boat. My legs are so wobbly I nearly fall when I first stand. And then I see him — up the bank just a little ways. He's got a military poncho that must have been in his truck strung between two trees and staked down in the back for a shelter, and he's tucked into his sleeping bag underneath, asleep. I have no way of knowing how long we've been here, how long since he paddled us to shore, how long since he crashed. I'm not about to wake him up. I'm hoping he'll sleep for the next twelve hours. There's no way we're getting back in time for me to get to school in the morning—which I'd already figured—so Jeremy might as well rest up. He probably needs this even more than I do—to get away from everything and finally relax.

And when he's done sleeping like he's dead, he can come back to life as the Jeremy he's supposed to be.

I dream about the wild pigs. They're still shot to pieces, still piled in the back of the truck, leaking, bleeding, dismembered, stinking. I'm trying to find the parts that go together—this leg to that bloated body, this head to that ragged neck, this jaw to that exploded face—though I don't know why it's so important. It's not as if I can bring them back to life. But I keep trying. And trying. Jeremy's not there, and I worry that he's been killed, too, and I'll have to find the parts of him as well and put them back together but, just like with the pigs, it won't be enough.

He's up before me. I know because I smell wood smoke and coffee when I wake up a second time in the gray light of early morning. Fog drifts off the river. I drag myself out of the canoe again, keeping the sleeping bag wrapped around me. It's mountain cold—the Blue Ridge rises up not far from the east bank across from us, and I shiver all the way over to a small fire and collapse next to it in the sand. The cookstove isn't on, but a small coffeepot is still warm. I find a tin cup and pour myself some. It's got grounds floating around in it, and it's black, but I don't care. It still tastes good and warms me going down.

Jeremy comes up from behind me and drops some wood next to the fire. He also has all our old bloody clothes with him.

"You're not planning to wear these again, are you?" he asks, sounding almost cheerful.

"No," I croak.

"Good," he says, and he starts laying items on the blaze, one after the other, starting with my jeans and T-shirt. Once those get going, he adds my jacket, then both our socks and underwear, and finally his fatigues. You'd think we were fugitives, shedding our old identities. Or we just broke out of prison and had to get rid of any trace that we were ever there.

The clothes smolder and turn the smoke black. Jeremy takes the now-empty coffee cup and refills it. He takes a sip and hands it back.

"You been awake for a while?" I ask, my voice working better now that I'm warming up.

"Not too long," he says. "Ground got a little hard after a while. You were lying on top of the air mattresses and I didn't want to wake you up to get one out."

"Sorry," I say.

"No worries," Jeremy says. "Drugs had worn off anyway."

"What drugs?" I ask.

"Some shit they give me for sleep. Ativan. Supposed to

knock you out. Supposed to cure anxiety, too. Supposed to do a lot of things."

"You said you didn't go to the psych eval," I say.

Jeremy takes back the coffee and finishes off the last swallow, which is mostly grounds. "Got it when I was deployed. They give that stuff out like candy."

"And it works?"

"Sometimes."

Jeremy pokes a stick in the fire, stirring the smoldering clothes so they'll continue to burn. Then he lifts the stick up to examine the red, glowing end.

"Annie says you have nightmares," I say. "She says that's why you can't sleep."

Jeremy pulls up his sleeve and lowers the stick so close the end singes the hair on his arm.

"Everybody has nightmares," he says. "Comes with the uniform."

He lowers the stick again but this time doesn't stop before it touches his skin. I can hear the burn. I jump up and knock the stick out of his hand. "What are you doing?"

He stares at his arm and then looks up at me. "We should get going," he says, but he doesn't get up right away. He picks up the stick and pokes it back in the fire, then looks at the long red blister already formed on his arm.

"Fuck, this hurts," he says, grinning. "What the hell was I thinking?" He grabs a water bottle and pours some water over the wound.

It's getting lighter out. The fog's starting to lift. I can see most of the way across the river to the other side.

"We're in this village," Jeremy says out of nowhere. "In this dream I sometimes have. Always the same piece-of-shit place — dirt roads. Mud houses. No electricity. No nothing. Except for goats. A lot of goats. We've searched it for weapons stashes, any sign of the fucking Taliban. We're getting ready to leave. I hear shooting on the other side of the village, where my men are, and I start running. But there're goats in the way. Herds of goats blocking the road. I try to push through them. Hammer at them with my weapon. I hear somebody crying, and I know it's one of my men, and I know he's been hit, and it must be bad because why else would he be crying. And I'm wondering why I hear just the one guy crying, and if that's a bad sign, that everybody else is silent."

Jeremy stops as abruptly as he started. He's sweating even though it's still chilly. He gets up and walks to the river's edge and sits down next to the canoe, practically in the water. I watch him for a while, to see if he'll do anything else or say anything else. He doesn't.

I stare down at my boots. All the clothes have long since burned up, but there's still blood on my boots from the wild pigs. Jeremy's, too. I don't think it'll ever come off.

20

We paddle in silence for a couple of hours. The sun's still not showing over the tops of the mountains, but it's light enough out that Jeremy's able to steer us around rocks and logs and, once, near the shallow west bank, a cow.

Out of the blue he says, "In the old days they thought that every river was evolving to a perfect state, to some kind of divine vision of what a river ought to be. Just like this river here. From up on the Blue Ridge it looks like the letter *S* copying itself over and over, like some snakes when they move, or like sound waves. They said it was what a perfect river was supposed to look like."

"They don't think that anymore?" I ask.

"No," he says. "It was just a pretty idea people had about how shit works. The grand design."

"Do you believe in a grand design?" I ask. I don't really know what Jeremy believes in. We hardly ever went to church growing up. Mom would take us sometimes, but the Colonel always said Sunday was his day to sleep in, and it was hard getting ready, tiptoeing around so none of us woke him up.

"A grand design?" Jeremy repeats. "No."

"What about God?" I ask, probably sounding like a dumb kid. "Do you believe in God?"

He spits in the river. "There's no God," he says. "And if there is a God, he sure as hell isn't in Iraq or Afghanistan."

And then he starts talking about dogs. Not good dogs — dogs we used to have, pets, that sort of thing. But dogs in the war.

"The first one I shot," he says, "was this diseased skeleton of a dog that kept growling at us while we were out of the Humvee, changing a flat. It kept inching closer, scratching and growling. Probably just wanted food, but we didn't want to get anywhere near the thing. One of my men asked if he could shoot it, and I said no. We were sitting ducks, out in the middle of nowhere, high mountains rising up on both sides with plenty of places for enemy to hide, the convoy backed up behind us, everybody nervous about us getting moving again. Goddamn dog kept inching closer, kept growling. One guy said there was saliva dripping out of the dog's mouth, like rabies, and they kept asking if they could kill it, and I finally got tired of hearing about it, and hearing the dog, so I pulled out my pistol and shot it myself. Clean shot through the head. And that was the end of that dog."

He pauses. "You hear stories about guys bringing home dogs they met over there, dogs that became their best friends and all that real heartwarming stuff." He shakes his head. "Not us. It was like we were determined not to leave any dogs in the whole damn country. We didn't even wait to see if the dog looked sick or diseased or starving or rabid or whatever. We didn't wait to see if it was acting aggressive, threatening, anything like that. If there was a dog hanging around a camp, it was a dead dog. If our convoy passed a dog on the side of the road, it was dead, too."

He paddles silently for a few minutes and doesn't say anything for a while. I have no idea how to respond.

"But big humanitarians that we are, we left the bodies there," he finally adds. "You know, in case the locals wanted to cook and eat that shit."

Sometime around what I guess to be midmorning, we pass the town of Strasburg. For the past couple of hours, we've been ducking under low-water bridges and, weirdly, having to maneuver around more cows that wandered down to the river from their farms up on bluffs on the left bank. Now there are some houses overlooking the river, and a lot more trash in the water than we've seen before: plastic and bottles and other shit that people throw there, or that washes down out of their yards.

I want to stop for breakfast, but Jeremy wants to keep going. "We'll pull off somewhere farther downriver," he says vaguely. Neither of us has had much to eat in the past two days, but we keep going.

A few miles after Strasburg disappears behind us, Jeremy picks up the river guide he bought back at the canoe-rental store. "Apparently we just passed Cedar Creek," he says. "Going to be a dam up here soon that we'll have to portage around."

He continues steering us clear of any rocks, even ones I can't see, not that I'm looking very carefully.

Instead, I check my phone, wishing I'd thought to do it when we were still in Strasburg. No service; I guess the mountains are blocking the signal.

I should be in history class right about now. We're studying America's wars, but it's all about generals and battles, winners and losers, maps and casualties and dates. Pop quizzes and time lines. Jeremy's wars are at the far right end of that history time line, hardly even there. Mr. Whelan, our teacher, says that in World War II, half of the families in America had a family member serving in the war. In Vietnam it was 20 percent. Now it's maybe 1 or 2 percent. He gets all worked up and says Call of Duty is more real to our generation than the real wars that are going on.

I wonder what Mr. Whelan would say if Jeremy came to history class and told that story about the dogs.

We haven't seen anybody else on the river all morning, probably because it's a school day, and getting chilly now that it's October, so Jeremy and I have it all to ourselves. The leaves have mostly turned, but there are still blazes of yellow and orange and red up the sides of the mountains. The water's low, but we're not scraping bottom, and only occasionally glancing off hidden rocks. I mumble "Sorry" for not spotting them, though I doubt Jeremy even cares.

We're both paddling now, so we're picking up speed. Pretty soon we come up on a small section of rapids. Nothing too challenging, but it takes all our concentration to shoot through it and not hit anything or tip over. The last section is a narrow sluice between two big moss-covered boulders. Jeremy lines us up like he's been doing this all his life and then tells me to paddle hard right until we get there. "Then use your paddle to push us away from the rocks if we get too close," he orders, and I do what he says as we rush down the sluice and through a small patch of churning water on the other side.

"Sweet!" Jeremy says, and just like that I'm grinning, too.

The river gets quiet again almost immediately and we're back to drifting.

"You know, the Colonel isn't a total asshole," Jeremy says, apropos of nothing.

I'm too stunned to do anything other than blink.

"I mean, yes, he *is* an asshole. But he's not *just* an asshole.

Just think about it," Jeremy continues. "Here's this woman with these two kids and no family to help her out. She's got a shitty little military pension coming after her fuckup of a husband dies. So this guy offers to take care of her and her kids — one of them not even out of diapers, and the other a certified jerk. About the only thing the guy knows is the Corps — giving orders and following orders. Semper fi. All that stuff. He never had much of a family either. Mom says he was kicked around between foster care and group homes until he was old enough to wear the uniform."

I'm gripping my paddle so hard I'm surprised it hasn't snapped in two. I can't believe Jeremy's trying to make me feel sorry for the Colonel, and be grateful that the Colonel moved in on Mom like he did, and took over our family.

"Why are you telling me all this?" I ask, not turning around because I don't want him to see how much I'm seething. All our lives, one of the things that bound me and Jeremy was hating the Colonel. Hell, he's the whole reason Jeremy had to go into the Marines, and fight in the wars, and is the way he is. He could have been playing football in college. He could have been doing a lot of things.

"I just think you should give him a break, is all," Jeremy says. "Think about Mom for a second. How would it be for her if he had another heart attack? If he wasn't around?"

"It would be better for her," I say. "There wouldn't be some son of a bitch ordering her around, putting her down all the time."

"I didn't say he was perfect," Jeremy says. "I just said maybe he didn't know how to do it any different. But Mom says he's gotten better since the heart attack, mellower."

I sit perfectly still, not willing to give him the nod of acknowledgment I know he's looking for. Because the Colonel *has* gotten better. I just don't think it's enough.

"You have to give him credit for being there," Jeremy says after a while. "That's all I'm saying. It ought to count for something."

"Well, it doesn't," I say.

"Someday you might feel differently," Jeremy says, like he's so wise now that he's a dad himself.

"I doubt it," I say.

21

Somewhere around noon, after portaging around a five-foot dam, we come to a campground. Jeremy, predictably, doesn't want to stop, but I insist. I tell him I have to take a shit, which happens to be true. But mostly I want to check my phone and let Annie know where we are.

Reluctantly, Jeremy eases us out of the current and over to the sandy bottom of a wide beach that fronts the campground. I drag myself out and pull the canoe up on land.

Even though I really, really have to go, I don't leave right away. My legs are stiff, for one thing, and I take a minute to stretch out. Jeremy climbs out of the canoe as well, and studies where we are — the slope up to the trees, the few campers scattered in the distance, a gray-block building that I'm guessing, hoping, is the bathhouse. He's probably sizing up where we're vulnerable to attack, defensive positions, escape routes.

"Everything OK?" I ask.

He takes a second away from his surveillance to look at me. "Weren't you going to take a shit?"

"Sure," I say. "Just, um, just wait for me. All right?"

He's back studying the terrain. "What the hell else am I going to do?"

"I don't know," I say. "I'm just saying."

"Well, just go already," he says.

The first thing I do once I'm in the stall is check to see if I can pick up a cell-phone signal. Thankfully I can.

I have a dozen new texts and another dozen voice mails. Guys on the team. Mom. Annie. There's even one from the Colonel, which surprises me: "I don't know what's going on, but your mother is so worried she can't sleep. Your little message just made her more worried, and this is unacceptable." He starts in about how I wasn't raised to run away from my problems, but I don't want to hear it. I hit delete. *Asshole.*

Mom doesn't sound all that worried to me in her messages. More like concerned. "I know you're with Jeremy, so you're OK, but you have school, Shane. You really shouldn't be missing class. Your stepdad is beside himself. And one of your coaches called the house. . . ."

Annie's left another message, but I call her back before I even listen to it.

"Hi, Shane," she whispers.

"Hey, Annie," I whisper back, before realizing that I don't need to. "You at work?"

"Yeah," she says. "In with the babies." Annie works on the pediatric ICU — Intensive Care Unit — at the hospital, where they have all the premature babies. I've been up there before. Most of them are in incubators. They're so tiny they don't look real, every one of them lying in a nest of tubes and wires and monitors and IVs.

"Can you talk?" I ask.

"Just for a minute," she says. "Where are you guys now, Shane? You said you'd be home yesterday. This isn't like you. Is Jeremy making you do this?"

"No," I say. "He isn't making me. We both just needed to get away from everything for a while."

"His CO called again," Annie says after a minute. "They're giving him a couple of days, but then . . ."

Then they'll come find him is what she doesn't say.

"I'll talk to him," I say. "We'll be home soon. Tomorrow, probably."

Annie sighs. "Shane, listen — Jeremy needs help. Real help. The kind you and I can't provide."

"He's fine," I say quickly. "He's just tired, is all. It's doing him good to be out here."

"You can't fix this," she says. "None of us can. You have to take care of yourself. You have to be careful, Shane."

"Nothing bad is going to happen," I say. "It's just Jeremy."

"Can you at least tell me where you are?" she asks.

But I don't want to say, for some reason. I don't exactly know who or what I think I'm protecting Jeremy from. Maybe the Marine MPs, if it's gotten to that point where they're even looking for him. But definitely not Annie. Of course not her. But what if she slipped up and said something to somebody . . .

"We're just camping out," I answer, which is true enough. "If you talk to Mom again, tell her that everything is fine. Just have her call the school and tell them I'm sick or something."

"Shane," Annie says, her voice still low. "I have to go, sweetie. Just promise me you'll take care."

"OK," I whisper back, as if my voice might actually wake up one of the babies at her end of the line. "I promise."

22

I know I should get back to Jeremy. He doesn't want to be here at this campground, and I know he'll be getting antsy. But the conversation with Annie leaves me unsettled, so after I walk out of the bathroom, I go sit on a nearby picnic table, out of sight of the beach, and call Hannah Marshall.

I don't really expect she'll answer since she's at school, and, sure enough, she doesn't. I can't think of what to say when it rings to voice mail, so I just hang up. I sit there for a minute, and I'm just getting up to go find Jeremy and the canoe when my cell phone rings.

It's her, calling back.

"Hannah?" I say, even though it's obviously her name on the caller ID.

"Yeah," she says. "I saw you called. Did you pocket-dial me or something?"

"Oh, n-no," I stammer. "Just thought I would call. Are you busy or something?"

She laughs. "I'm at school. Of course I'm busy. Where are you? Aren't you supposed to be in class?"

"I'm skipping today," I say. "Mental-health day."

"Oh. Well, that explains why I didn't see you in the cafeteria at lunch."

"Were you looking for me?" I ask, surprised.

"No," she says. And then, "Sort of. You never came back on the field after that spectacular run and all — which, of course, everybody's been talking about. And somebody said you might have gotten a concussion during the game. I was just hoping you were all right."

"Are they really still talking about it?" I ask. It feels like Friday night was ages ago, though I guess to everyone back at school it's still fresh news.

"Yeah. Sorry," she says. "So did you get one?"

"Did I get one what?"

She laughs. "Maybe that answers my question. Short-term memory loss is supposed to be one of the signs, you know."

"Oh," I say. "The concussion. Yeah, I think so. I didn't

go to the doctor or anything. It was no big deal. I probably could've kept playing, but I was too embarrassed."

"I know the feeling," she says.

"Yeah, but probably not too many people saw yours," I say. "Mine was in front of the whole school."

"One of the perks of playing a sport no one cares about," Hannah says.

"So where are you anyway?" I ask. "I mean, it's not lunch anymore."

"Well, I was in class," she says. "And then you called, and so I came out in the hall and called you back. And now I'm in the bathroom, sitting on a toilet."

I laugh. "I was just doing the same thing."

"You're calling me from a bathroom?" Hannah says.

"Well, no. I'm sitting at a picnic table now. But I was just in the bathroom talking to someone else."

"Oh," she says.

"It was just Annie," I say. "She was worried about Jeremy," I add in a rush. "We're kind of on this trip together, in the mountains. But he lost his phone, and so he couldn't call her to tell her he's OK."

"I saw him at the game," Hannah says. "He was by himself."

"Yeah. He's not big into crowds these days."

"Somebody told me he gave a pretty weird pep talk or whatever to you guys a couple of Fridays ago."

"It wasn't weird," I say. "Whoever said that is a dick."

I know I sound defensive. But the thought of people making fun of Jeremy pisses me off.

"So is everything OK, Shane?" she asks, her tone more serious.

"Oh, yeah, sure," I respond, too quickly.

But she doesn't press me. "It's nice that you called," she says instead. "I was hoping you would. Though I didn't really expect it after I was such a bitch when you helped me with my flat tire."

"No, you weren't," I say. "I guess I deserved that — what you said and all. I should have called you before or something."

She's quiet for a minute. "So why *did* you call, Shane?" she asks, that seriousness back in her voice.

"I don't know exactly," I say, which is the truth. "I just appreciated that you left that message. And I just kind of wanted to talk to somebody."

I don't know what to say after that, and apparently neither does she. We share this silence for a minute. I can hear her breathing, and she can probably hear me, too.

"I guess I better go," I say, finally. "Thanks for calling me back."

"Sure," she says. "I better go, too. Back to class and all that."

"So maybe I'll see you?" I ask.

"Sure," Hannah says. Then she adds, "Be safe, OK? Don't fall off a mountain or anything."

23

Jeremy has taken the M16 apart and laid all the pieces care-fully on a tarp in a secluded spot hidden from the campsite by a thick copse of trees. He has a clear view of the river and the sandy beach and the canoe, but it takes me a minute to spot him when I return after making my calls. I guess that's the idea.

"Hey," I say.

"Hey," he grunts. A minute later he has the M16 back together and we're easing back down to the boat. Jeremy climbs in first and lets me shove off.

"That was one seriously long shit," he says.

"Diarrhea," I say back, and he lets it go.

The next few hours are kind of fun as the river picks up speed and we paddle through rougher water. It isn't anything like serious white water, but I have to keep my eyes peeled for obstructions. No more cows, thank god, but still plenty of boulders and logs to snag ourselves on or slam into.

We can see more houses now through trees lining the river, and I figure there must be a road up there above the left bank, judging from the sound of cars. We pass a couple more campgrounds but still don't see anyone else on the river. We don't talk the whole time, except for me telling Jeremy where he needs to steer around stuff, but that's OK. I'm tired of talking. I just wish I could shut off my brain as well.

The mountains recede to the east, though we can still see them. The October sun burns higher in the sky, and we strip off our jackets and then our sweatshirts. I roll up my pant legs and take off my bloodstained boots. I stop paddling briefly to dangle them in the water, but not very much of the blood washes off, not even when I rub hard.

For a while things get rural again. No houses anyway, or none that we can see. We pass a couple of old ford sites, where dirt roads still lead down to the river from either side. Jeremy says they're from colonial times and the Civil War. "Sheridan, the Union general, had his men destroy everything in the valley," he says. "Torched fields, slaughtered livestock, you name it. If it could be killed, he killed it. And old George Armstrong Custer — around here is where he wiped out the Southern cavalry and turned himself into a celebrity killer. Getting a hard-on for the Indian Wars out west once there wasn't anybody left around here to put down."

"Thanks for the history lesson," I say, not in the mood for anything at this point except something to eat. But despite his earlier promise, Jeremy hasn't mentioned stopping again.

By midafternoon, probably five hours since we passed Strasburg, the trees thin out again, and farms and pastures on both sides of the river give way to more houses. The river curves even farther away from the mountains, which makes me depressed. I like having them there, looming over us to the east. They make me feel sort of protected. I guess Jeremy feels the same way because he goes into hypervigilance mode, head constantly turning to check his flanks, to stare down whatever might be up on any bluff to the west, behind any boulder or tree stand onshore.

More buildings. More cars. More garbage in the river. More traffic noise as we draw nearer to Front Royal, where the North and South Forks will finally come together to form the Shenandoah. "This sucks," I say.

"Gonna suck worse in a minute," Jeremy answers, and sure enough, next thing I know, there's another five-foot dam that we'd be idiots to try to paddle over, so we pull up onshore, haul everything out of the canoe, then drag our gear around the dam and go back to portage the canoe. Jeremy's limp is more pronounced than it was earlier. Likely from sitting in the canoe so long, but who knows? I can't be sure he's been taking the antibiotics they gave him at the hospital in Manassas, but I know better than to ask.

Though there is something I have to bring up. "How about lunch?" I ask. "You said we'd stop somewhere."

"Not here," Jeremy says, throwing our gear back into the canoe on the downside of the dam. "Little ways farther. I want to get away from town."

"But town's where we're going to find food," I point out.

A Jeremy order is a Jeremy order, though, so I wait for him to climb in — gingerly, it seems to me — and then I shove us off again into the current and the Front Royal trash floating along with it. A mile or so later we reach the confluence forming the full-on Shenandoah, but it doesn't do much for the scenery, which gets worse if anything. Dust drifts down on us from some sort of plant up on the left bank. I can hear the roar of big machinery up there but can't see it, thanks to sycamore trees still lining the bank.

I slip my cell phone out of my pocket to check the time, and notice that I have a signal here. I have a sudden urge to call Hannah again, which is funny, since before this week it'd been months since we'd talked to each other. I remember her telling me her dad had a drinking problem, and that back when we were in middle school, he lost his job and they lived in a trailer for a while. Maybe she would understand a little bit about Jeremy, about how I'm worried about him but don't know how to help him, other than to be on this crazy trip with him.

But not now. I put the phone away and we keep paddling.

I'm just about resigned to the certainty that Jeremy is never going to let me eat, that we're never going to get off this river for so much as a quick dash to a convenience store for a Coke and a package of crackers. But then, without saying anything, he steers us over toward the shore. It's just a little ways north of some sort of industrial plant. He studies his guidebook for a minute and then takes us up a small creek I almost didn't see, hidden behind small, thick brush on the left. He says it's called Crooked Run.

"This says there's a golf course up there." He points in the general direction of the bank and a small bluff. "It's a country club. Should be a clubhouse where we can eat in style."

"But we're not members," I say.

"Don't worry about it," he says. "You want to eat, we'll eat."

Jeremy climbs out of the boat, and the first thing he does after that is grab the M16 and roll it inside the tarp. Then he stashes it in some brush twenty feet away, throwing sticks and leaves on top so that in a minute I wouldn't suspect anything was there if I didn't already know.

"What about everything else?" I ask.

"Leave it," Jeremy says. "Pull the boat farther up out of the water."

While I'm doing that, he checks the 9mm and then tucks it into its holster. When he pulls on his jacket again, it hides the gun.

So that's it, then. I guess it's finally lunchtime.

24

Jeremy walks toward the country club like he owns the place. I scurry along behind him, wondering what the hell he's up to. He strides across the golf course, right through the middle of somebody's game. When they yell at us — they're still back up on the tee; we're halfway down the fairway — Jeremy just waves and keeps walking. When they continue yelling, he kicks one of their golf balls into the rough.

"You're going to get us in trouble," I say.

"Doubt they even saw it," he says back.

We cut across another fairway, a putting green, around a couple of sand traps, and up to the clubhouse.

It's like the guy who's been living in our basement, who doesn't even want to stop at a campground so I can use the toilet, has vanished, and Jeremy's back to being his old cocky self.

Though he does insist on a table where he can have a chair backed up against the wall.

"Beer for me, Shirley Temple for him," Jeremy says as soon as a waitress approaches.

"Very funny," I say.

The waitress laughs. She's young, somewhere between my age and Jeremy's. Pretty, with blond hair pulled back in a ponytail, wisps of it escaping down the sides of her face. She wears golf clothes, but I'm willing to bet that she's in jeans and T-shirts when she's not at work. Her name tag says "Amy."

"I don't think I've seen y'all before," she says in a distinct Virginia drawl.

"First time here," Jeremy says. "Just joined."

"OK," Amy says, sounding skeptical but still smiling. "Well, do you have your ID cards yet? Or know the number, at least? I have to have that on the order."

Jeremy leans over the table toward her. She leans forward, too. "Here's the thing," he says. "I lied. We're not members. Just hungry. Figured there wouldn't be a crowd in here this time of day. We've been paddling on the river. My little brother hasn't had anything to eat in days. If you can take care of us without saying anything, we'll take care of you on the bill. I promise."

135

He lays a ten-dollar bill on the table and slides it over to her. She looks around for a second and then takes it, tucking it inside her apron.

"You been deployed?" she asks Jeremy.

He nods. "What gave it away?"

I think she's going to say something about his military haircut. She doesn't. "It's your eyes and all," she says, her smile fading a little. "My boyfriend looks just like that."

"He a Marine?" Jeremy asks.

She shakes her head. "Army Reserve. They sent him over for a whole year. Driving supply trucks."

"How's he doing?" Jeremy asks.

"Still driving trucks," she says. "Back here now. It's for a gravel company. He does this funny thing, though. Always has to check underneath before he gets in to drive, even if he just stopped for gas. I guess he's checking for bombs."

"Not surprised," Jeremy says.

"Yeah, I guess if you've been there, that sort of thing gets normal and all," she says. "He checks under the bed, too."

"Bombs?" I ask.

"Maybe," she says. "Or the bogeyman."

She pulls out her order pad. "Well anyway, I'm glad y'all came in. What can I get you? Whatever we got in the kitchen, it's yours."

Jeremy doesn't eat much. A few bites of a hamburger. Couple of fries. He does put away three beers while we're there. I barely have time to take notice, though, and I don't say anything, busy as I am, stuffing myself. Once I'm through with my plate, I pull his over and finish off what he hasn't eaten.

Amy checks on us a couple of times to see if we need anything else. Eventually Jeremy asks for the bill.

Amy grins. "No charge. One of the members put it on his account."

I look around. Except for a couple of golfers I can see through a door in the next room at the bar, we're the only ones here.

"Was it one of them?" I ask.

She shakes her head. "He isn't actually here today. Just scrawl a signature on here, messy enough that nobody can read it." She slides the bill over to Jeremy. The ten he'd given her earlier is tucked underneath.

"No," he says. "You keep that."

"Uh-uh," she says, shaking her head. "You can put a tip on the bill, though, if you want."

"Sure you're not going to get in trouble for this?" Jeremy asks. "Rich people don't like people taking their money."

"This one won't ever notice," Amy says. "Plus he's a dick."

Jeremy shrugs and signs. He tips her twenty, and also leaves the ten on the table. We take off before she sees it and insists on Jeremy taking it back.

"Glad we stopped?" he asks as we traipse back across the golf course.

Before I can answer, we run into the guys from before, the ones who yelled at us for cutting across their fairway.

They stop their cart far enough away that we're no physical threat, but near enough that we can hear them.

"You're not supposed to be here!" one yells. "Don't think we're not calling Security, because we already did."

A second one holds up his cell phone.

"Calling again right now to tell them where you are!" he shouts.

We're standing next to a sand trap. Jeremy nods and smiles at the guys, then he unzips his pants right then and there and pisses into the sand.

The guys immediately start flipping out, yelling over one another, sounding like the Tower of Babel. I just stand there nervously, wanting to take off running but knowing there's no point if Jeremy's not with me.

Jeremy, all nonchalant, finishes his business, zips back up, and waves to the guys again. They're all red-faced from screaming at him.

"Always wanted to do that," he says to me, sauntering across the fairway and back toward Crooked Run.

I'm sweating, wishing he'd walk faster, but Jeremy's determined to take his own sweet time, almost as if he wouldn't mind Security catching up to us.

"I'm just glad you didn't decide to take a shit," I say.

He snorts. "Maybe next time."

I check my cell phone once we're back on the water. There's a text from Hannah. "Glad you called. Call again if you want."

My battery is low, and I wish I'd thought to ask Amy back at the clubhouse if she had a charger I could use.

I offer it to Jeremy. "Why don't you call Annie?"

He won't take the phone. "What for?" he says.

"You know, check in, let her know you're OK. Tell her when you'll be home."

"I'm betting you already snuck in a call to let her know what's up, so no use me doing it a second time."

"She's your wife, Jeremy," I snap. "Just fucking call her already."

Jeremy has been smiling and good-natured since we stopped at the country club. That changes.

"Watch it," he says, a serious edge to his voice.

I put my phone away and turn back toward the river.

It seems like we're barely back in the canoe when we have
to pull out again and portage, this time over a much higher
dam, probably twelve feet. I don't know where we are,
exactly—Jeremy hasn't said—but there's a power plant on
the bank, and we have to wade through a tangle of bushes
with all our gear, the canoe resting on our shoulders
upside down.

"Slow the fuck down!" Jeremy barks when I storm ahead,
pulling him too fast behind me on his bad leg.

It's late in the afternoon, and I'm about done with this
river. Ready—more than ready—to go home, no matter

what is waiting back there: the pissed-off Colonel; worried-sick Mom; Coach and my teammates, who I'm sure are done with me, too; a disappointed Annie, who I can't help feeling I've failed in some way, going along with Jeremy on this trip, which is now stretching toward the end of the third day with no end yet in sight.

We stumble down the rocky bank and through sticker bushes that tear at our clothes, back to the river. Jeremy sits on a flat rock and pulls off his pants. Then he peels the bandage from his wound. It doesn't look good — red, pus-filled, swollen.

"Jesus, Jeremy!" I exclaim, not able to help myself. "Haven't you been taking the antibiotics?"

He doesn't answer. Just pulls out antiseptic wipes and cleans everything up, then slaps a thick wad of gauze over the seeping stitches and tapes it tightly to his thigh.

"It's nothing," he says when he's done. "Let's get going."

"Get going where?" I ask, but he ignores me. Stupid pack animal that I am, I haul the rest of our gear into the boat, hold it steady while he climbs in, then push us off again into the current.

The Shenandoah is a lot wider now that we're past the confluence, both forks poured in together, plus the various other creeks and runs and tributaries adding to the volume. It's maybe 150 feet across in this section, but still faster than the North Fork. My shoulders ache from all the paddling we've done since leaving Woodstock.

As dusk comes on, we pass Morgan's Ford Bridge and

have to duck down to get under — so low that if I'd left my head above the sides of the canoe, the bridge would have given me another concussion. After that, the river widens even more, with a lot of mild rapids, which keep things bumpy, though not too exciting. No white water or anything. Just a hassle to steer through. The banks rise high on both sides, the left lined with a thick forest of sycamores, and as it gets darker, it feels as though we're passing through a tunnel. We ram hard into things a couple of times, jarring my teeth and giving me a headache. Jeremy still won't stop, though.

He seems driven now, refusing to slow down his paddling or to let me slow down mine. "Come on, you pussy," he says more than once. "I'm doing all the goddamn work here."

Instead of telling him to fuck off, I work harder. He's my older brother, and I'll probably always be trying to prove something to him, even when we're so old the only thing we can race is wheelchairs.

Deep in the night, maybe around midnight, we pass under the Route 50 bridge, and after that, the river goes flat and clear — so clear that when the moon breaks through the cloud cover, I can see down to the sandy bottom in some places. The mountains have returned to hug the east bank, as if they're growing right out of the river, once again protecting our right flank.

Maybe that's why Jeremy relaxes a little, slows down his paddling. I don't ask him. I just say "Fuck it" and stow my paddle in the canoe. "You're on your own," I say to the darkness. "I quit."

142

Jeremy doesn't answer, and I lean back on our gear the way I did the night before, making myself as comfortable as I can. I zip up my North Face jacket, pull my knit cap tight over my ears, jam my hands deep in my pockets, and close my eyes.

"Wake me up when we get there," I say, with no idea when or where that might be.

Jeremy paddles. He steers. We drift. I fall asleep, wake up, fall asleep again, wake up again. I hear owls and splashes in the river that aren't Jeremy's paddle.

Once when I wake up, we're drifting backward down the river. Jeremy must have dozed off, but I'm too tired to turn around and look.

I fall back asleep and dream about Mom and the Colonel. Someone is yelling at me. I must have messed something up. Only it's not the Colonel this time. It's Mom, her face dark with rage, demanding to know what I have to say for myself. But I can't speak. I try and try, but nothing comes out. I have to get to Annie's house, but I can't tell Mom that either. But I have to. Annie needs me, and I have to be there, but no words will come out. None.

I hear the sounds of metal against metal. It has nothing to do with my dream. It's the thing pulling me out of that frustrating dream.

I open my eyes and there are stars, so many stars, thousands of them, no light to crowd them out of the night sky. A perfect bowl of ink-black night punctuated by those stars.

And the metal sounds continue, behind me, forcing me to finally sit up and turn around to see what's making the noise.

It's Jeremy, his paddle nowhere I can see. He's got the M16 apart and he's putting it back together. Then taking it apart again and putting it back together again. And a third time. Or the third that I've seen.

But who knows? Maybe he's been doing this all night and I just slept through most of it until now.

His eyes are squeezed tightly closed the whole time he works. That's the other thing, the unnerving thing, more than his obsession with the gun.

Even blind to everything around him, everything else in the world, he still knows what to do with that M16.

26

When I wake up in the morning, we're on an island.

I don't know this at first, of course. At first I don't know anything except once again I'm alone in the canoe, dragged up on a narrow sandy beach. Like on the morning before, Jeremy has set up a lean-to with his tarp on the shore where he's sitting next to a fire. I smell coffee again, just like yesterday morning, and stumble out of the boat to get some.

Jeremy has the M16 in his lap, just lying there like it's his baby. He has the 9mm out, too, and he appears to have been cleaning that as well.

"Did you sleep at all?" I ask, reaching for his cup to pour it full for me.

"A little," he says. "Not much. Got too tired to keep paddling, so pulled up here."

I burn my tongue on the coffee. "And where exactly is here?"

He gestures with the 9mm at the opened guidebook. "Parker Island. Middle of the river. Fucker must be a mile long. We're just a little ways past Castlemans Ferry, if that helps."

I take another sip—and burn my tongue again, goddamnit. "Not really," I say. "I've never heard of Castlemans Ferry."

"How about West Virginia?" Jeremy asks.

"Yeah," I answer tentatively.

"Because another mile or so and that's where we'll be," he says.

"And then where?" I ask. I wish I'd paid more attention in whatever class it was where we learned about Virginia geography, though I'm doubting we covered much on West Virginia anyway.

"Harpers Ferry," Jeremy says. "Some kick-ass white water up that way. Thought we'd check it out."

I finish off the coffee and pour myself some more. There's not much left. "Might as well, since I've probably been expelled from school by now."

"Oh, please," Jeremy says. "They won't expel you for missing a few days. Just get Mom to tell them you were in the hospital on account of your concussion."

* * *

Every part of me hurts when we shove back out into the river and pick up our paddles. I work out all the time on the football team, and even when we're not in season — running, lifting, swimming. One time back in the spring, when Hannah and I were going out, we rode bikes over to Lee Drive and all the way out to where they have three Civil War cannons and a stone pyramid to commemorate the Confederate soldiers who died in their trenches, holding off the Union advance in the Battle of Fredericksburg. It took us a couple of hours to get there and back. If we had kept going out, there's no telling how good I might have gotten on the bike. I'd probably be doing triathlons by now.

Paddling again after two days of it, though, and a couple of nights of not enough sleep and days of not enough food, I feel so weak I wonder how I ever managed to do any of that, much less hold my own on the football field. I keep thinking I'll loosen up after we're on the river for a while, but an hour later, I hurt worse than ever. I even catch myself groaning. It's probably totally beautiful here on the water — Indian fish dams; rocky bottom; a couple of empty landings; another long island in the middle of the river; the gray of morning giving way to a brilliant blue sky — but it's all lost on me.

Jeremy doesn't groan, of course, and his paddling is as steady as it's been since we left Woodstock a hundred years ago. He's still steering us expertly down the river, over ledges, around obstructions. I don't know how he can even see anymore, as little as he's eaten and as little as he's slept.

"Is that where we're going to eat next time?" I ask him, hoping conversation will help. "Harpers Ferry? Because I'm starving."

"Works for me," Jeremy says. "But it's going to be a while."

This I don't want to hear. "How come? How goddamn far is it?"

"Not far," he says, studying the guidebook. "But we're going to have to get off the river up here a little way. You see how wide the river's getting? There's a big power dam up here — Snyder Hill Dam. Twenty-footer. Supposed to be all fenced off. No way over and no way around."

This I don't want to hear either.

"Don't worry about it," he says, anticipating whatever complaint I'm about to utter. "I'll figure something out."

As if on cue, the river opens up into the widest section we've been on yet. Jeremy says they call it the Big Eddy — slow and deep and wide and flat. A lake, basically. He says they also call it No Man's Land.

"But killer white water once we get past all this," he says. "All the way into Harpers Ferry."

I splash too hard with my paddle. Cold water comes back in my face. "Yeah," I snarl. "So you already told me."

"Why do you keep taking apart that gun?" I ask Jeremy after another silent half hour. The sun is higher now, well over the mountains. It's a hot day for October. "I heard you doing it last night in the canoe."

148

"I don't know what I was thinking, laying the parts out like that," he says. "If we'd capsized, I would have lost it all."

"So why were you doing it?" I ask again. "Like, a bunch of times."

"Keep in practice," he says. "Always ready."

"For what?" I know this conversation isn't going to go anywhere, really. Jeremy probably doesn't know himself why he's so OCD about the gun. Or maybe he does. Maybe that's the Marine way. Except that we're not on some patrol or mission or whatever. We're on this river in Virginia — in *West* Virginia — that's so peaceful they write songs about it.

"Hard to explain," he says at last, "but all that time over there, patrols and shit, even inside the wire, you just don't feel safe without your weapon. Without every weapon you've got. And if you ever need it, it better by god work right or you're dead, and you're the only one who can make sure of that."

"Would you go back?" I ask, since Jeremy suddenly seems to feel like talking.

"That desert shit hole? We're done shooting up that place. They can kill one another off if they want — and apparently they do — but we're out of there."

"What about the other war?"

"In a heartbeat," Jeremy says. "In a fucking heartbeat."

"Because we're winning?" I ask.

Jeremy laughs one of his bitter laughs, and I know that was a stupid, little-kid thing to say. "We're not winning," he says. "They're just waiting us out, same as they did the

Soviets, same as they did the British. Only one way to ever win a war with them."

"Which is what?" I'm back to paddling steady again. So is Jeremy.

"You ever read *Heart of Darkness*?" he asks. "It's about the Congo in Africa. Guy named Kurtz is supposed to be this great missionary type, only things don't work out too well. It's a novel. Takes place a long time ago."

"No," I say. "Never heard of it. What about it?"

"Couple of famous lines near the end," Jeremy says. "In one of them, Kurtz has written this really long, detailed, bureaucratic report on the situation with the locals — the natives — only when they find it, he's scrawled over the top of some of the pages: 'Exterminate the brutes.'"

"Jesus, Jeremy." The way he says it gives me chills. One minute it sounds like he hates the war so much that he can't even bear to be around other Marines. The next minute, like now, it almost sounds like he loves it.

I'm hesitant to ask about the other line, but I'm also curious, so finally I do.

Jeremy doesn't respond at first, and we keep paddling until I almost forget I asked. But then I hear him behind me, this disembodied voice speaking in a sort of stage whisper, echoing over the water.

"'The horror. The horror.'"

27

We're nearly past the couple before I see them, up on the bank, partly hidden by trees. We're in sight of the dam at the north end of the Big Eddy, fast running out of room. The guy is fishing, or trying to. The girl finishes off a can of beer and then opens another. She throws her empty in the river.

The guy barks at her. "Goddamnit, Glory. I told you not to do that. You're scaring off the goddamn fish."

Whatever she says back I don't hear.

Jeremy steers us over toward them. The guy looks up but doesn't say anything. The girl, Glory, waves.

"Hey, y'all!" she says, her voice loud. "Where you going?"

We're maybe twenty feet away, back-paddling to stay still and not run into the guy's fishing line. "Trying to get down-river," Jeremy says.

The guy still doesn't acknowledge us. Glory takes a long drink of her beer. "You better not try to go thataway," she says, pointing toward the dam. "Ain't no way to get past all that."

"Thanks," Jeremy says. "We were hoping we could get a ride. Wondering if you have a truck up there, maybe give us a lift with our canoe. Just far enough so we can put in past the power plant, closest point of access."

"We just got here," Glory says.

"No, we didn't," the guy says. He pulls in his line. "How much?"

"How's twenty bucks?" Jeremy asks. I'm busy looking up and down the bank, hoping there's somebody, anybody, who we might ask instead. I don't like the looks of these people. The guy has a huge wad of tobacco stuffed in his cheek, and he spits every ten seconds. Glory's T-shirt hangs so low in front that I can practically see her whole bra. Plus she's obviously drunk, even though I doubt it's much past noon. He looks thirty. Glory looks a lot younger.

"Fifty," the guy says.

"Kind of steep," Jeremy responds. "Can't be that far. You'll be back here fishing in an hour."

"Seventy-five," the guy says. He spits toward our canoe. He's not exactly sober either. There must be half a dozen empty cans next to him on the ground.

"How about if we pay you thirty dollars?" I say, splitting the difference.

Jeremy lets us drift closer, not seeming to care about the fishing line anymore. The guy spits again, almost hitting my paddle.

"A hundred," he says. "Take it or leave it."

I look over at Jeremy, hoping he's not getting worked up about this. But he's busy pulling all the money he has out of his wallet. "Only have about eighty in here," he says. "You can have that or drive us to an ATM so I can get more out of the bank."

Jeremy's actually reaching toward the guy with the money. The guy smiles, showing off his black wad of tobacco. He takes his baseball cap off, holds it by the bill, and extends it out toward Jeremy. Jeremy lays the money inside and the guy pulls it back in.

The girl, Glory, is wide-eyed. "I get half, right, Danny? It's my truck, so I get half."

Danny doesn't take his eyes off us when he responds. "Yeah, but you don't have a license now, do you, Glory? Anyway, I'm the one made the deal." Then to us he says, "I ain't helping carry that canoe up the bank, or none of your stuff either. The deal is just to drive y'all and that's it."

Jeremy paddles us all the way over to the shore. I step out and pull us up on the bank and start unloading the gear, dumbfounded that Jeremy is going along with this creep.

Glory is still whining at Danny about the money, about her half.

"I already told you," Danny says. "You're not part of the deal."

"Then, fuck you," she says. "You can't use my truck."

Danny laughs. "I have the keys, dummy. What are you gonna do, take 'em away from me?"

I busy myself hauling the gear up a steep path to the top of the bluff, wishing there was some way to turn down the volume on the Danny and Glory Show. They're still yammering away at each other, her bitching at him, him alternately ignoring her and telling her to shut the hell up.

Jeremy and I have to drag the canoe up the path — the trees are too dense for us to carry it on our shoulders — and once we're all the way up, we carry it another fifty yards to a small clearing next to a gravel road, where we load it onto a surprisingly new, shiny Ford F-150.

"I can't believe you paid him so much!" I say to Jeremy. "That's like extortion or something."

He shrugs. "It's just money. No use getting bent out of shape about it."

We climb down the bluff to get the rest of our gear. Danny and Glory are still going at it by the river. Things seem to be getting heated. Their voices are louder. Their faces red.

"It's my damn truck, Danny!" Glory shrieks in his face. "I shouldn't have to give you any of the money."

Danny glares down at her, but Glory doesn't seem intimidated, even though he's a foot taller than her. I guess being drunk helps.

"I made the deal," he says, keeping his voice even. "End of story."

Danny turns his head to spit a thin stream of black tobacco juice on the ground, but some lands on Glory's shoe.

"You spit on me!" she yells. "What the hell?" She pulls off her shoe, staggering on one leg for a second, then wipes it on Danny's shirt.

He recoils. Looks down at the tobacco smear. Then, without saying anything, he takes off his baseball cap and hits Glory with it across her face, hard. She ducks away but he follows and keeps hitting her with the cap — on the back of her head, on her shoulders, on her arms as she raises them to block him. "Stop it, Danny! Goddamnit, I said stop!"

I don't even see Jeremy move, he's just suddenly there, grabbing Danny's arm and pulling him away from Glory, who falls on her butt in the sand and just flops there like a rag doll, sobbing.

Jeremy has Danny by the throat with one hand. With the other, he takes the cap and tosses it on the ground. Danny's eyes are wide, frantic. He looks like he's struggling to breathe.

"I'm going to let you go now," Jeremy says, "but you're going to have to calm the fuck down. Now promise me you'll calm the fuck down. Can you do that? Just nod your head."

Danny nods and Jeremy lets him go. Danny folds over, hands on his knees, gasping.

I'm still frozen at the base of the bluff, where I'd been standing with Jeremy when all this started. Jeremy turns to Glory. "You OK?" he asks, but she doesn't answer. She's crying too hard, still just sitting there, legs splayed, arms hanging limply by her sides.

Danny straightens up, coughs, picks up his hat, and jams it back on. Then pulls out a saw-edge fish knife from a leather sheath on his belt.

"Jeremy!" I yell, pointing.

Danny lunges, thrusting the knife at Jeremy, but Jeremy is quicker. He lifts both his arms, easily blocking Danny's knife hand, then, in one motion, whirls around, pulling Danny's knife arm forward and trapping Danny's arm at his side. He pulls Danny so close that the guy is pressed against Jeremy's back, flailing at Jeremy with his free hand, or fist, though he can't get any leverage and Jeremy ignores the weak blows. Instead he focuses on locking his right hand around Danny's wrist so he can't do anything with the knife except wave it uselessly in the air in front of them.

Then, once he's got Danny's knife arm securely trapped, Jeremy hammers his left elbow into the guy's stomach, doubling him over. When Danny's head drops forward, Jeremy slams an elbow into his face — once, twice, three times.

Blood explodes from Danny's nose. He drops the knife and collapses onto the ground.

Jeremy picks up the knife, throws it as far as he can into the river, then walks back over to Danny, who's writhing in the dirt, both hands pressed over his face as if he's trying to collect all that blood. Jeremy kicks him hard in the ribs and Danny howls.

"Stay down now and we might be done here," Jeremy says.

Glory's not done, though. She's been watching everything sort of in a state of shock, like me, but now she shrieks out something incomprehensible, struggles back to her feet, and launches herself at Jeremy — though it's a slow launch as she staggers through the sand.

I intercept her before she can get to him, though, grabbing her from behind and holding on tight while she screams and struggles.

"You bastard!" she yells at Jeremy. "You killed him! You killed Danny!"

Jeremy just looks at her and shakes his head.

"Take it easy," I say. "He was just trying to help you."

She answers by reaching back and clawing at my face. Her fingernails are sharp and she draws blood. It hurts like hell.

So I throw her in the river.

Ten minutes later, Jeremy and I are in Glory's truck, bumping down a rutted set of tire tracks until we hit a narrow two-lane road with a dividing line so faded it might as well not even be there.

"Holy shit, Jeremy," I say as we bounce onto the pavement. He's driving. I'm still hyperventilating. "That guy . . ."

"Yeah," Jeremy says. "I hate drunks."

"Drunks with knives," I say. "And psycho girlfriends."

"Them, too," he says, slowing as he steers around a curve so the canoe won't slide in the bed of the truck.

"You were just trying to help her," I say, repeating what I said to Glory.

"No good deed goes unpunished," Jeremy responds, as if it's no big deal.

"Are you OK?" I suddenly think to ask. "I mean, he didn't get you anywhere with his knife, did he?"

Jeremy laughs. "That guy? Not a chance. Looks like the girl did worse on you."

I feel my face where she clawed me. It's still bleeding a little.

"Should have let her drown," I say. It took us forever to get her out of the river, not that she was in any danger, as shallow as it was where I threw her in. But I guess if she'd waded farther out, it was possible she could have gotten swept up in the current, such as it was, and gotten carried over the dam or something.

Danny just lay on the ground the whole time, whimpering. Jeremy didn't even ask — he just reached in Danny's pocket and took the keys. When we finally coaxed Glory back onshore, half lifting her, half trying to stay out of reach of her claws, she pushed us off and staggered over to her boyfriend. She practically flung herself on top of him, sobbing, saying, "Are you OK, baby? Are you OK?"

Danny pushed her away. "Goddamnit, Glory!" he barked. "You're getting me all wet!"

That was when we grabbed the rest of our gear and left. Jeremy didn't even say anything, and I just followed him — back up the bank to the top of the bluff. We took the truck.

* * *

159

We pass the power plant on the right shortly after heading up the paved road, and once we're past, Jeremy tells me to look for a road or tire tracks or anything off to the right that might take us back down to the river. "There's supposed to be a long rock bed below the dam," he says. "High cliff on the right bank — that's why we couldn't portage on that side. But the river should be accessible here shortly."

Sure enough, we come across a dirt road off to the right, and when Jeremy takes it, we're back to the river almost immediately. And no bluff to negotiate down to the water.

"Sweet," I say. "But what about the truck? Shouldn't we take it back?"

"They know where we're going, so they'll know where to look."

"OK," I say. "I guess."

"Don't worry about it," he says. "Let's just get back on the river already. This is supposed to be the best section for white water and rapids — here to Harpers Ferry. Should be great."

I'm not so sure about just leaving the truck, but what are my options — make Jeremy wait here while I drive the truck back and then walk all the way here?

Jeremy's limp seems worse as we muscle the canoe out of the truck bed and down to the water, and I can see there's blood soaking through his jeans.

"I'll get the rest of the stuff," I say, and for once he doesn't argue with me about it. Instead, he eases himself down and leans against a tree hanging over the water. We can see the dam and hear the loud rumble of water over the rocks below it, though where we're about to put in is calm. Fast-running, a lot narrower than above the dam, but calm.

It takes me a few trips to get everything from the truck. Jeremy had wrapped the M16 inside the tarp so Danny and Glory wouldn't know we had it and get freaked out or anything. It's one of the last things I bring back from the truck. I unroll the tarp and just stand there for a minute holding the weapon, feeling the weight of it, wondering if a guy like Jeremy, totally trained, can tell the difference when it's loaded and when it's not.

Right now it's not — the magazine is in the tarp — but I still have this urge to toss it in the bushes. Or sneak down to the river and throw it in there. I can't even say why, except that it makes me nervous for us to have it. For Jeremy to have it. Of course he still has the 9mm tucked away somewhere. He would still be armed. But standing there I have a sort of flashback to the wild pigs, all that carnage in the field where Jeremy blasted them the other night, whenever that was.

I suddenly can't remember what day it is, and how long we've been gone, and I realize it's been a long time since I thought about home, thought about Mom and the Colonel, Annie and the kids, the trouble I'm in when I go back. The trouble Jeremy will be in if he doesn't report soon for his psych eval. It's as if all that belongs in another world, another life almost.

My cell phone still has some battery left, and I think about calling home but then don't. Instead I send Hannah Marshall a text. "Hey. If you ever want, maybe we could go canoeing sometime."

I start to text more, but there's too much to say, and too much I guess I shouldn't say. At least not right now. Not until this whole adventure is over or whatever.

I leave Glory's keys in the ignition, and then, probably because I've watched too many cop shows on TV, I wipe everything down so, hopefully, we won't leave any finger-prints. Just in case. Too late I notice a bloodstain on the driver's seat where Jeremy was sitting, and no matter how hard I rub, I can't get that out.

I take the M16 and head back down to the water.

"Damn, you're slow," Jeremy says when I get back with the last armful of stuff. He's holding a small bottle of some kind of whiskey.

"Found it in the truck," he says before I can even ask. He offers it to me. "Want some?"

"I thought you hated drunks," I say.

Jeremy takes a drink. The bottle is only half full, but without knowing how much was in there when he found it, I have no way to tell if he's already had a lot or he's only just started.

"I do," he says. "Doesn't mean I hate drinking, though." He caps the bottle, slides it into his pocket, checks on the

9mm in its holster on his belt, then pulls himself up to standing. I can tell his leg has stiffened up since he's been sitting there by the way he drags it behind him over to the canoe.

"We're gonna need to wrap everything really well in the tarp," he says. "And lash it to the yoke and the thwarts."

I just look at him. "What the hell are you talking about? What yoke? And what are thwarts?"

He points to the three crosspieces between the seats that I guess hold the sides of the canoe together. "These here are the thwarts," he says, pointing to the two straight pieces. "The one in the middle with the curved parts, that's called the yoke. It's the balance point. If you're portaging by yourself you can lay it over your shoulders and hold on to the grips."

I have no idea how Jeremy knows this stuff. We never did any canoeing growing up that I can remember. And I doubt they spend a lot of time in canoes in the Marines. But it's always been this way with Jeremy — him knowing a lot about a lot: how to work on cars, how the Earth came to be, how to throw a curveball, why they call it the *theory* of evolution and not the fact. About the only thing he didn't know how to do was stay out of trouble with the Colonel. Though I guess he probably could have figured that out, too. He just didn't care.

I don't ask any more questions, just get busy doing what Jeremy says, wrapping everything up tightly, lashing it to the thwarts and the yoke.

"What about the M16?" I ask.

"Tuck it deep inside as far as it'll go," he says.

Just before we shove off again into the Shenandoah current, I check my phone to see if Hannah might have texted me back. But down here on the water I can't pick up a signal.

29

Jeremy says they call the next few miles of river the Staircase — because it drops so fast in such a short amount of time. I don't believe it at first because for about a mile or so we're still just paddling in flat water, though we do hit a few rapids, dropping over small ledges and squeezing between a few large rocks jutting out of the water. Not exactly an adrenaline rush. It's late afternoon, but the sun's still warm, sky's still blue, shore's still green.

Then, suddenly, we round a bend and hit a quick-water stretch that has us going almost sideways for a second, then shooting over a ledge that runs diagonally from the right bank of the river upstream to the left bank downstream. The Shenandoah narrows even more there, funneling us through a narrow passage that drops so fast and so hard that the bow of the canoe dips under for a second and then throws water all over me as it breaks back up, bucking wildly.

Before I can so much as catch my breath, we're shooting through another passage so narrow that the wall scrapes the side of the canoe — and my knuckles, holding tight to my paddle, when I don't pull my hand back in time. There's blood all over my hand, but the water crashing up from the rapids washes it off just like that.

"Keep paddling!" Jeremy yells, though I can barely hear him over the cacophony of the churning river. "Push us off that rock!"

I'm about to yell back, "What rock?" but there it is, looming right in front of me, and just in time I manage to push us off, afraid my paddle will splinter from the force of it. I dig in after that, pulling hard with each stroke, though I'm not sure why we would want to go even faster.

We blast through a third narrow passage and then a fourth, and I'm betting we've dropped three feet in just the past hundred yards or so — the length of a football field — and then we're out of it, or sort of out of it anyway. Just enormous rocks to maneuver around, but that's something we can handle OK. I realize I'm panting, and whatever adrenaline rush I wasn't having before when we got on the river, I'm having plenty of it now.

"Pretty sure this is Bull Falls!" Jeremy yells, though I can hear him OK now that the river has widened a little.

"What's next?" I yell back.

"The Bull's Tail," he says, and before I can ask, "What?" we're back in it, big waves and white water and another ledge rapid, but it turns out that that's just the warm-up to three hundred yards of quick water as the river gets funneled to the left and we drop suddenly over what looks like the remains of an old dam, and which I don't see coming until we're flying over it.

"Holy shit, Jeremy!" I yell, or whoop, or something. He whoops back — as excited as I am, I'm guessing, though probably not as scared. For the next mile or so the river is totally nuts, dropping us over one ledge after another, some of them so high I can't believe we're not flipping over. I see one ahead of us that looks like a goddamn waterfall, and I start screaming back at Jeremy, "We have to stop! We have to stop!"

But of course there's no way to stop, and then it's too late anyway, and we're in this white, churning sluice, banging off rocks, drenched in foam and spray, the bow dipping so low I'm afraid I'm going to fall out, but then we bang out of it and sort of bounce back and right ourselves, and I'm about to do one of those enormous sighs of relief, when — holy shit again! — there's another one!

I'm dimly aware that we're under a bridge as we hit it, or as it hits us, and I shut my eyes this time because I'm so freaked out, and it feels as if we're in the air, flying, and then we hammer back down into the water so hard it makes my teeth ache, and the next thing I know, Jeremy is steering us over to the shore, laughing his ass off—whether at me for flipping out or at the river for that crazy, crazy ride, I don't know.

"Paddle hard or we'll end up in the Potomac!" Jeremy yells, still laughing, and I realize we're at the confluence of the two rivers—the Shenandoah and the Potomac—with a railroad bridge practically right overhead. I dig in hard on the right side, and with just a couple more strokes, we're there, at a sort of landing between the two rivers.

I jump out of the canoe, but my legs are shaking so bad I can barely stand. Somehow I manage to stay upright, though, and even pull the canoe up.

Jeremy lifts his paddle with both hands over his head, in celebration or whatever. "Welcome to Harpers Ferry, Shane. Looks like you might have survived."

We carry the canoe farther up onshore, above the rocks to a grassy shelf bordered by trees—not exactly hidden from anything, but Jeremy decides it's OK. For a while.

Cars driving over the bridge we passed under have their headlights on, though it's still light out, not quite dusk. Jeremy and I pile our gear on the tarp. He tucks the M16 under the canoe, then eases himself down beside it and pulls out the bottle of whiskey he rescued from the rednecks' truck. There's still some left; he makes half of it disappear.

"How's your leg?" I ask.

He waves his hand as if brushing the question away. I let it go.

"How about getting something to eat?" I ask. "And maybe we can find somewhere to stay? My back is pretty sore and stiff."

Jeremy takes another drink. "Sure," he says. "Whatever." But he doesn't make a move to stand up or do anything. His adrenaline rush seems to have vanished, but I'm still amped up, pacing in front of Jeremy, hopping from one rock to another.

Four more boats — a kayak and three of those yellow rubber-looking dinghies — come racing down the river, shooting out of the rapids the same as we did. The guy in the kayak barks orders, and the others steer over to shore not far from us, though I don't think they see us. They leap out and dance and yelp. Their guide just smiles and busies himself picking up life preservers and gear.

They carry their boats up to a parking lot. I decide to follow them, though far enough behind that they don't take notice. They busy themselves lifting their boats onto a trailer that's waiting for them, and in just a couple of minutes more they're gone. I knew we were close to Harpers Ferry, but I didn't know how close: the town is pretty much right across the street.

I go back down to tell Jeremy, but of course he already knows.

"So let's go eat," I say. "It's starting to get dark, and I'm hungry."

"Didn't you just have a burger — and most of my lunch, too?"

I can't tell if he's joking. "That was yesterday."

"That how long it's been?" Jeremy asks. He slurs his words, just a little, but I notice.

"Come on," I say. "You can't survive on a liquid diet."

Jeremy finishes off the bottle. "Oh, I don't know about that. How about you go and bring me back something. I'll camp out here for now."

I try talking him into going, but he won't budge. He flicks a credit card at me. "Should be enough room on here for a hamburger or whatever. And a couple of beers for me."

"I'm underage," I say. "Can't buy beer."

"Are you kidding me? No fake ID?"

"Sorry to disappoint."

He shakes his head. "I'll pick something up later."

I trudge back up the path to the parking lot and across into Harpers Ferry, which seems to have been built on the side of about the steepest hill in America. I feel like I need handrails to haul myself up the streets, and I wonder why the whole place doesn't just slide right down into the river.

30

I duck into the first restaurant-looking place I come to — it's hard to tell what's what in all these old historical buildings. It would be a great place to eat if I was hungry for scented candles. The next place is an ice-cream shop, so that's a little better. A girl behind the counter smiles at me when I walk in. She's probably my age, wearing a dumb antebellum dress I'm guessing they make her wear to work there. Even so, she's kind of pretty, except for a chipped front tooth.

"Hey," she says. "Want some ice cream?" She was out sweeping under little round tables and metal chairs when

I walked in but slips behind the counter now and waves a scoop, as if to prove she can dish up some as soon as I give the word.

"Actually, I'm looking for real food," I say. "Sorry."

"What kind of real food? We have chili." She points at the blackboard on the wall behind her, where all the ice-cream flavors are listed. In the corner it says "Homemade Chili" and "Hot Dogs."

"How old?" I ask.

"They made it at lunch," she says, pointing now to a slow-cooker on a counter behind her. "It won an award."

"It won an award today?" I ask.

She laughs, and there's that chipped tooth again. "No. Just in general. For, like, best chili in Harpers."

"What's in it?"

She shrugs. "I don't know. Chili stuff: Meat. Peppers. Spicy stuff. Onions."

"Okay," I say. "I guess I'll try some."

She smiles. "You're the first customer all afternoon," she says. "So you get as much as you want. They'll probably just throw the rest away anyway."

She tells me I can sit anywhere, and a minute later she brings me an enormous bowl of chili, a bunch of crackers, and a hot dog.

"Uh, I didn't order a hot dog," I say.

"On the house," she says, plopping down ketchup and mustard. Then she goes back for all the stuff you're supposed to bring out first: water, a spoon, and napkins.

"Usually people just get ice cream," she says. "Anyway, dig in. It won't hurt you, I don't think."

"Sounds pretty appetizing," I say. But soon enough I'm wolfing down the chili, which is surprisingly good for something that's been sitting in a slow-cooker all day.

She stands and watches me the whole time. "Boy, they hadn't fed you in a while, had they?" she asks.

"Sorry," I say. "And no. We've been canoeing. Me and my brother, Jeremy. Haven't eaten since yesterday afternoon."

"Where y'all from?" she asks, pulling out a chair and sitting at my little round table.

I tell her, and she tells me she's from Shepherdstown, which is ten miles away, and that she's a junior in high school and she can't wait to get out of West Virginia.

"It must be great to live so close to Washington. Do you go there all the time? What's there to do where you live? Are you guys staying the night in Harpers Ferry? Where's this brother of yours anyway?"

I can't tell whether she's flirting with me or just bored, but I keep up my side of the conversation between bites because it's nice to have a banal conversation with somebody after so many days with Jeremy.

"I'm Dawn, by the way," the girl says at some point. "We don't wear name tags."

"Nice to meet you, Dawn. I'm Shane."

"Shane, huh? I never met too many Shanes."

"It was the name of a character in an old movie," I explain. "My mom said my dad really liked it."

"What's it about?" she asks, seeming genuinely curious.

"It's a Western. This drifter named Shane gets hired by a farmer and ends up protecting the guy's family from bad guys. He kills all the bad guys, but he gets shot, too, only he rides away on his horse, so you don't know if he lives or dies. It ends with this little kid who sort of idolizes him, running behind Shane and his horse, yelling 'Come back, Shane!'"

"Does he?"

I shake my head. "Doesn't look like it."

Dawn frowns. "I hate people like that," she says.

I'm not sure how to respond. I'm just about through with the chili. The hot dog is still waiting. It's gray — that color hot dogs get when they've been cooking in water for a long time.

Dawn asks me a bunch more questions, definitely flirting now: What grade am I in? Why aren't I in school? Do I have a girlfriend? I say "Sort of" to the last question, which is a stretch, because I couldn't say that Hannah Marshall is even sort of my girlfriend.

She gives me that chipped-tooth smile. "Doesn't look like 'sort of' came along on your trip with you," she says, getting up from the table. Then she punches me on the arm.

As soon as I finish the chili, Dawn refills the bowl and sets it down on the table with more crackers. She refills my water and asks if I want a milk shake. "Any flavor," she says. "Go ahead, pick one."

"Surprise me," I say.

She grins. "You asked for it," she says, grabbing an ice-cream scoop. "I'll do it with my eyes closed."

And sure enough, she keeps her eyes tightly shut as she fumbles from one ice-cream tub to the next, throwing whatever she happens to scoop into the blender cup. I'm pretty sure there's pistachio, mint chocolate chip, some kind of red sherbet, and I have no idea what else.

She opens her eyes to fit the cup under the blender, then brings it over. "Here you go, Shane."

"Thanks, Dawn."

At first it tastes really interesting. Kind of good, actually. And then, after a few swallows, it switches to bad, and then pretty quickly to awful. Dawn must see it on my face, because she starts laughing. "Let me have a taste," she says, pulling it over in front of her. She takes my straw in her mouth, which sort of surprises me and sort of doesn't.

"Oh, yeah," she says. "That's disgusting."

It's my turn to laugh. I have to admit I'm enjoying just being stupid in this ice-cream shop with this girl, though there's still a part of me saying I should get back soon to check on Jeremy. I've already been gone an hour. Not that he's probably even noticed, as drunk as he already was when I left. But still.

I ask Dawn if she happens to have a cell-phone charger that will work on my phone, and she says yes. "It's in the back," she says. "I can go get it." She pauses and looks at the front door. "Or you can come back there with me," she adds.

I know that if I follow her back to the storeroom, I won't be leaving anytime soon. But I really do need to charge my phone. . . .

I push back from the table and follow her. She pulls a charger out of a shoulder bag and hands it to me. She pulls out something else, too: a joint.

"Want to get high?" she asks. "While we wait for your phone to charge?"

"I don't know," I say. "I should probably be getting back."

She frowns. "You hired guns are all alike," she says. "You ride into town and get everybody all worked up, then just ride off into the sunset."

I stare at her blankly for a second.

"You know," she says. "Like that movie you told me about? *Shane?*"

I can't exactly leave now, so I follow her to the back of the shop and we stand there with the door open, sharing the joint. Dawn takes really long, deep puffs, while I pretend to do the same but take in only a little smoke each time.

"Aren't you worried somebody will come in while we're doing this?" I ask, kind of late.

She lets out a long stream of smoke, and coughs. "Middle of the week," she says, as if that explains it.

After a while we sit down on the back steps. The town seems really dark, as if the black-ink night is absorbing the pale yellow from the street lamps. There's no evidence of life in the alley behind the shop, just the usual Dumpsters and wood crates and pallets and debris.

"So what do you think?" Dawn asks from really far away. I turn to see where she's gone, but she's still sitting right next to me, which is weird. My mouth feels too funny for me to say anything back, so I just grin. It could be I'm just staring at her, slack-jawed, because she keeps looking at me expectantly. I'm obviously not keeping up my end of whatever exchange is supposed to be going on.

A cat appears from somewhere and comes up on the steps and sits down at my feet. I reach out to pet it, but Dawn grabs my arm. "He'll scratch you, the little bastard," she says, sounding really far away again. "He just wants food."

I pull my arm back. Dawn still has her hand on me, and I stare at her fingers, which look bigger than normal girl fingers. I put my hand over them to cover them up, but she must think it's something else because she leans in and kisses me, which also feels really strange. I kiss her back, of course, because that's what you do in a situation like this. And then we're making out right there on the steps. Eventually she pushes me away and stands up and pulls off her antebellum dress.

I'm expecting to see a bra and panties, but she has on shorts and a T-shirt, which for some reason makes me laugh. She doesn't seem to care, though; she sits back down and wraps her arms around me and pulls my face back to her face and we start making out some more. I'm wondering where this might go next — where we might go next — and then we hear somebody calling out, "Hello? Hello? Anybody back there?"

Dawn jumps up and I practically fall down the stairs on top of the cat, who is still sitting there, waiting for food. "Damn!" she says, pulling her shirt down and fumbling for her uniform in the half dark of the storeroom. "Damn!"

She gives up and just brushes her hair out of her face and wipes her mouth with the back of her hand and goes up front to wait on a middle-of-the-week customer.

Five minutes later I'm back at the river — at both rivers, where the Shenandoah pours into the Potomac. But there's no Jeremy. And no tarp or sleeping bags either.

I dive deeper into the trees, calling his name. I run up to the parking lot but can't find him. I work my way up the bank, following the Shenandoah, searching the shore and the rocks by the river, but still nothing. I'm cursing Dawn for keeping me so long — refilling my food, getting me high, distracting me — even though I know I can't really blame her.

Back at the canoe I search through everything, looking for a clue — something, anything, that will tell me where he could be. I splash cold water on my face, trying to clear my head and figure this thing out. Where the hell would Jeremy go? And then I realize — the guns! The M16 is gone, and so is the 9mm, which he always keeps on him. Suddenly I'm in a panic that Jeremy might have gone off somewhere to hurt himself.

But why take the sleeping bags? Why take the tarp?

I sit in the sand where Jeremy had been sitting on the tarp and life preservers when I last saw him. The empty whiskey bottle is there, sticking up out of the sand where he left it. I stare at the amber glass, turn it around in my hands, and realize something's been scrawled on the label. It's too dark to read what it says, so I follow the light to the parking lot, where I stand directly under the street lamp and see clearly what's written there — what Jeremy wrote there.

Just two words: "Jefferson Rock."

31

I stumble back up the steep Harpers Ferry streets to the ice-cream shop. Still too stoned to think very straight, I can't set my sights on where else to go for directions, even though it occurs to me that Dawn might be a little mad that I took off earlier without saying good-bye.

She's standing behind the counter, glaring at the front door, when I walk in, as if she's been expecting me. She waves what looks like a bill, and before I can speak, she says, "You left without paying."

"I'm sorry," I say. "Really. I am. I was just — everything got kind of confusing there, and I had to go check on my brother."

"I thought you were a nice guy," she says, still holding out the bill. "I wouldn't have kissed you like that if I hadn't thought you were a nice guy."

I close the door behind me. I'm anxious to find out where Jefferson Rock might be so I can find Jeremy, but I don't want to piss Dawn off any more than I already have. "I *am* a nice guy," I say. "At least I try to be. I really didn't mean to run off like that. I wasn't thinking straight. Anyway, here." I hold out Jeremy's credit card. "It's Jeremy's, but I can sign for it."

She takes the card, studies it for a minute. "Jeremy Dupree." She glances at me. "So you're Shane Dupree?"

I nod. She doesn't say anything else. Just goes to the register and runs the card and brings me back the receipt. She's charged me for two orders of chili, the gray hot dog I didn't order and didn't eat, the milk shake, even the crackers. I tip her the cost of the order, then sign Jeremy's name.

"My brother," I say when she hands me my copy. "He went somewhere called Jefferson Rock."

"So?"

"So I was hoping you could tell me where that is. So I can find him."

She puts one hand on her hip. She's still just in shorts and her T-shirt. "Why are you so worried about your brother anyway?"

"I don't know," I say. "He just got back from the war."

"And?"

"And nothing," I say, unable to hide my frustration.

181

"Look, can you help me or not, Dawn? I already said I was sorry, and I am. But I have to find him. *Now.*"

"All right," she says. "It's just that you hurt my feelings, taking off like that. And I sort of have a boyfriend, too, just so you know."

"I didn't know," I say. "Sorry again."

She waves her copy of the receipt with my generous tip. "I guess it's OK."

Then she tells me how to get to Jefferson Rock. It turns out to be not very far — a fifteen-minute hike up a steep set of stairs, past a church, down a path, into the woods, on the top of a hill overlooking the valley. "You can see just about everything from up there," she adds. "Where the rivers come together. The railroad bridge. The cliffs on the other side."

"Thanks, Dawn." I turn to go.

"Wait," she says. She holds up my cell phone. "You left it in the back. It's all charged." She smiles and there's that chipped tooth again. I remember the feel of it when we kissed before.

"I might have put my number in your contacts," she adds. "In case you come back sometime."

I hold out my hand and she holds out hers, and we shake, which is a weird thing to do after you've just made out with somebody. Then I lean down and kiss her again — on the cheek — and then I'm gone out the door, cutting across the street, and climbing the first set of stone stairs to Jefferson Rock.

* * *

I'm out of breath well before I get there. Hands on knees, I bend over, gasping for air, wondering how the hell I ever got so out of shape, or if it's the pot, or just fatigue from everything that's happened the past however-long since Friday night when I got the concussion.

When the roaring subsides in my head—the blood rush, the rasping breath—I hear, faintly, Jeremy's voice. I straighten and look around, but I don't see him. All I see are trees, and the faint outline of the path leading forward.

I strain to figure out where his voice is coming from, and what he's saying. It's the Lord's Prayer of all things.

"Our Father, which art in Heaven, hallowed be thy name, thy kingdom come, thy will be done on Earth as it is in Heaven. Give us this day our daily bread and forgive us our trespasses."

He pauses there, then repeats the line: "Forgive us our trespasses." And again: "Forgive us this day for our trespasses. Oh, fuck, right. Forgive us this day. Forget us this day. Forget us this night. And deliver us from evil. Deliver us more evil."

He's drunk. That's all. Just drunk and babbling. I push on down the trail, turning this way and that way, hearing him, then not hearing him. I step out into a clearing, and it's just as Dawn described it: the sudden view of the rivers, the cliffs, the railroad bridge, the tops of the trees, the lights. A big slab of rock sits on pillars on top of an even larger rock. I'm guessing one of them must be Jefferson Rock. But I still don't see Jeremy. I don't hear him now either.

183

I skirt the edge of the clearing, wondering if there will be park rangers or anybody up here at this time of night — whatever time of night it happens to be. I nearly step on Jeremy before I see him, deep in the shadow of trees.

He grabs my pant leg. "Wondered when you'd get here," he says.

I squint into the darkness. He's got the M16 in his lap, the tarp and sleeping bags dumped beside him. He has a six-pack of beer, too, the bottles all standing at attention in their cardboard sleeves. At first I think he hasn't started in on them yet, but then I see all the bottle caps are off. I pick one up and turn it upside down.

Empty. They're all empty.

"Didn't save you any," he says. "Since you're underage and all."

I sit down beside him on the damp ground. "Why'd you come up here?"

Jeremy slides his hands up and down the M16, just checking it, I guess. "Too much exposure down there. Easier to defend up here."

I don't know if he's kidding or serious. Probably both. "Were you thinking we'd sleep here?" I ask. "I'm pretty sure this is, like, a national park or something. We might get in trouble."

"We'll just pull back a little ways farther in the shadows," he says. "Plenty of cover here." He doesn't wait for me to agree. He pulls himself up and grabs a sleeping bag and the

M16 and the tarp and drags them back between two trees. Then he spreads the tarp and lets himself down on it and leans against one of the trees.

"How's your leg?" I ask.

"Will you just shut up about the goddamn leg?" he snaps, and I know that means it's bothering him. If it weren't so dark, I'd probably see more blood seeping out of the wound. I have no idea how he managed to hike all the way up here.

"So, uh, Jeremy," I say. "I was just wondering about tomorrow."

"What about it?" He's still cradling the M16, his eyes closed.

"Any idea about how we're going to get back? Do we just call the guy and he comes from Woodstock and picks us up, and the canoe, and takes us back to get your truck?"

"Good question," Jeremy says, not opening his eyes. "I'll give him a call in the morning."

"You can use my phone," I say. "I got it charged. This girl let me use her charger."

Jeremy looks at me. "Girl, huh? That what took you so long? Good for you. Annie told me you don't go out much. Didn't know you were saving it up for West Virginia."

I'm embarrassed. "I wasn't saving it up. Anyway, there's a girl back home." I check my phone, which I haven't had time to do since leaving the ice-cream shop. "She texted me."

"Who did?" Jeremy asks. "West Virginia or Back Home?"

"Back Home." Hannah wrote that I could call her tonight. If I wanted.

"I feel kind of guilty or something," I say. "Hanging out with this girl I just met."

"Is she your girlfriend?" Jeremy asks. "The one back home."

"Not really," I say. "We went out a couple of times when you were deployed. But I kind of was too busy — helping Annie, and spring football, and school. Everything."

"I don't think you have anything to feel guilty about," Jeremy says, sounding like a real big brother. "I mean, if you think there's some sort of, you know, mutual understanding with Back Home, then that's different. But it doesn't seem like it."

"Yeah," I say. "Thanks." This is nice. I'm not sure I can even remember the last time we had a moment like this.

And then it's over. Jeremy hands me the M16. "You get first watch," he says. "I'm crashing."

"What am I supposed to do with this?" I ask, trying to refuse the gun.

"Stand guard, dipshit." He doesn't bother to crawl inside his sleeping bag; he just unrolls it and pulls it over him. "Wake me up in a couple of hours and I'll take over."

32

Jeremy actually falls asleep. I can tell by the snoring. You'd think they'd train them in the Marines not to do that. If we were somewhere in combat, he'd be giving away our position for a mile all around.

The M16 feels cold in my hands. I wonder what it would feel like to shoot something with it. I had the opportunity, of course. Those wild pigs, the ones Jeremy shot and told me to finish off. But I couldn't.

I check my phone again after he's been out for a while. There's a message from Mom wanting to know if I'm all right and when I'll be home and if Jeremy is OK. A guy on the team texted and said he hoped I wasn't wandering around

DC or something, lost, with amnesia from the concussion. Ridiculous stuff like that.

Finally, there's a really short text from Annie. She's saying a prayer for me and a prayer for Jeremy. And then there's this: "Please just bring him home safe, Shane. Please."

I don't know why, exactly, but it hits me hard when I read it: How much she loves him. How scared she is.

How stupid I've been.

I look at Jeremy's face as he sleeps. He's all sharp lines and shadows, as if he's in pain all the time, which maybe he is. Sometimes he twitches, sometimes he moves his lips and makes sounds that aren't quite words. Maybe he's saying the Lord's Prayer again, or that twisted version of the Lord's Prayer I heard earlier, disembodied, in the woods. I think about Annie's face and how beautiful she is, but also about how there's always been a deep sadness there, too. I can't remember it not being there — in the set of her eyes, in her own thousand-yard stare — except maybe a long time ago, when I was little, back before Jeremy's first deployment. I'm pretty sure they were happy then. I'm pretty sure she was happy.

And I think about that bruise, and how I don't want to admit that Jeremy could have had anything to do with it. How many times had he told me that we weren't ever, ever, ever, going to turn out anything like the Colonel — and the Colonel hadn't even ever hit Mom, not as far as we knew. What had Jeremy done when he went home to talk to Annie after their fight?

I ease up off the ground, lean the M16 against a tree next to Jeremy, and slip out of the shadows to that barren patch of stone that holds Jefferson Rock. I ignore the keep-off signs and sit with my back against the rock, looking out on Harpers Ferry spread out below me. I wish I could call Annie and just talk to her. But it's too late, of course. And something about this trip with Jeremy has made her seem too far away.

I text Hannah instead. "Hey, it's me. Are you awake?"

She calls me right back. "Where are you? I mean, hi, Shane. Sorry. But where are you? Oh my gosh, everybody's been wondering."

"Still on the river," I say. "Well, we're pulled off for the night, but you know what I mean."

"You're crazy," she says, laughing. "Aren't you worried about getting into trouble for skipping all this school and everything?"

"Trying not to think about it," I say. "Anyway, how are you? What's going on back there?"

"Same as yesterday, pretty much," she says. "Basketball practice, school, homework. Fending off questions about the mysterious missing Shane."

"People were asking you about me?"

I can practically hear her shrug. "Just a few people. I didn't tell them anything, though."

"Thanks."

She's quiet for a minute. "This is all kind of funny, don't you think?"

"What is?"

"I don't know," Hannah says. "Us. Talking like this, more than we ever did when we were dating. Don't you think that's pretty weird?"

"I guess," I say. "I hardly went out with anybody else since you and I went out."

There's another pause on her end. "Why did you say that?" she asks.

"I don't know," I say. "I just thought you might want to know."

"OK," she says. "So what does 'hardly' mean?"

"Oh, boy," I say. "Nothing, really. Just a couple of times I went to the movies. With somebody. But then I didn't go out with them again. I wasn't interested. It just was awkward." I'm babbling, but I can't seem to stop, until she interrupts.

"It's OK, Shane," she says. "You don't owe me an explanation or anything. We can just talk about what's going on now. It doesn't have to be about ancient stuff."

"OK," I say. "Thanks."

She asks me how Jeremy's doing. "I've been thinking about you and him," she says. "Wondering if everything's OK. You said that Annie was worried about him . . . ?"

She says that last part like it's a question, I guess maybe expecting me to tell her that I'm worried about Jeremy, too, that he's gone psycho or something.

"He's fine," I say, my jaw tight. "He just wanted us to go on this trip, since he's been deployed so much and we haven't gotten to spend much time together in such a long time."

"Right," she says, and I can tell just from how she says that one word that she knows there's a lot more to the story than I'm letting on.

Jeremy is sitting up when I get back, the sleeping bag draped over his shoulders. Even in the dark I can tell his eyes are bloodshot — from drinking, fatigue, lack of sleep, one of his nightmares . . .

He's holding the M16. "Should have figured you'd pussy off somewhere when you were supposed to be doing a job," he snarls.

I just stand there, caught off guard. Earlier Jeremy was playing the part of the good older brother, even though he was drunk. Now he's back to just being a big asshole.

Part of me — the dumb-little-brother part — wants to apologize for messing up, even though I didn't really. Another part of me wants to tell him to go fuck himself.

I do both. "Sorry," I say. "And fuck you."

I brace myself for how he'll respond. But he just laughs.

I crawl inside my sleeping bag and try to fall asleep on the rocky ground. But it's cold, and eventually I'm shivering so bad that Jeremy, who's sitting up with the M16, keeping watch, tucks his sleeping bag over me, and drags me on top of the tarp so I'm not directly on the ground. I'm so frozen and so tired that I don't even think about what he's going to do to stay warm.

At one point, hours later, something wakes me up. I peer out from my sleeping bag and see him out on the open expanse of rock, pacing back and forth between that precariously balanced Jefferson Rock and the precipice over the river valley. He's limping, muttering to himself, holding tight to the gun. The moon has melted him and the M16 together and turned them both to silver.

"Jeremy," I whisper. He doesn't hear me. And then louder: "Jeremy. What's going on? Are you OK?"

He stops, changes directions suddenly, and comes over. Using the gun like a crutch, he eases himself to the ground, his bad leg splayed out to one side. He presses on the wound and winces, then he leans toward me.

"Here's a story for you." Now he's the one whispering. "It's some shit I never told anybody. You want to hear it?"

"Maybe we should both just get some sleep," I say. "You can tell it to me in the morning."

"I'm not tired," he says, and then he starts his story. "Over there, about the worst thing you can do is fart when you're a guest in somebody's house. You're not supposed to fart at all where anybody can hear you, but especially not when you're in somebody's home. It's this cultural thing. Very, very bad. They talk about how people have gotten killed for farting, no shit. They're big into respect and honor and all that. So no matter what, when you're a guest, you have to eat whatever they serve you — and eat all of it — and you have to not fart. And did I mention how much greasy food they have over there, and how many beans they eat?"

"This is bullshit," I say.

192

"No bullshit," he says. "You can look it up. Go ahead. Pull out your phone and look it up."

"No reception," I lie, too tired to bother fact-checking him.

He nods, and presses his leg again, and winces again. It occurs to me that he's not doing it to test anything. He's doing it because he wants to feel the pain.

"So here we are in this one guy's house, this elder," he continues. "We're supposed to convince him not to sell his crop of poppies to this warlord we've been trying to bag. They buy up all these farmers' crops and turn them into heroin, these warlords. It's how they finance their operations, buy weapons, pay for the materials for their IEDs. Only we can't touch the fields. Don't want to alienate the farmers. So we offer to buy it instead. I've got wads of cash to hand out to these fuckers. So this one, he's got his wives cooking all day for us, and we have to sit there for hours, stuffing ourselves, and every time we finish one thing, they bring out something else, or more of what we just ate. It goes on and on like that — the old guy, the elder, just sitting there watching us, all of us eating with our fingers, getting all greasy and getting disgustingly full. I'm trying to talk business and my translator is translating between bites."

Jeremy stops abruptly, like that's the end of the story.

"So what happened?" I ask, wondering if he forgot what it was he was talking about. "Did somebody fart?"

"Yeah," he says. "Somebody farted. One of our guys.

He asked my permission, and I said no. I told him I didn't care if his intestines exploded, but he was not allowed to fart under any circumstances. He held it in as long as he could. He practically shit his pants. But the point is, it happened. And it wasn't quiet either. Nothing you could pretend was something else. It was one of those loud, long ones, like someone was running a fucking lawn mower. The old guy, the elder, got this look on his face like we'd just shit in his food—which probably wouldn't have been nearly as bad of an insult. I went right into offering him the money for his crop, but he ignored the translator and just glared at my Marine—him and his sons, who were also there and also pissed. Finally we all stood up to go. I thanked the old guy a bunch of times, but he and his sons still didn't say anything, and we finally just left."

"What happened to the poppy field?"

"Oh, well, we torched it."

"They didn't try to stop you?"

"Couldn't," Jeremy says.

"How come?"

"One of the sons came after us for insulting the old man. Things got out of hand."

I blanched. "You *killed* him?"

"He had a weapon. It was either kill him or let him kill my Marine." Jeremy's voice is monotone, matter-of-fact. But he hesitates before saying the rest. "Like I said, they're big on honor over there. Once one of the sons got dead, the others came after us. And the old man. So they all got dead, too."

33

Jeremy's still awake, still holding on to his weapon, when I get up in the morning. I have no idea how I managed to sleep after his story. It took a long, long time.

I drag myself out of the woods, trailing tarp and sleeping bags and everything, and join him at the base of Jefferson Rock. The sun hasn't yet crested over the far wall of mountains across the river, but it's getting light out. Jeremy grunts but doesn't say anything at first, doesn't even look at me, even when I drape his sleeping bag over his shoulders. Maybe he's so stiff from the cold that he can't move.

I sit on the tarp and pull my sleeping bag as tightly around me as I can and wish I was little again and could lean against Jeremy, or even crawl into his lap, like I did when I was really little. He never told me I was too old to be doing stuff like that. And it always felt like the safest place in the world, like nothing bad could happen so long as Jeremy was there to protect me.

"In the Civil War, after some of the battles," he starts, as if we had just been in the middle of a conversation, "they would find rifles that had been loaded two or three times, sometimes more, but never fired. A lot of them."

"So?"

"A lot of soldiers — the majority — weren't regularly firing their weapons," he says. "That's the point. They were pretending to shoot. Then reloading so it looked like they were firing. But they didn't want to kill anybody. Even though they were getting shot at themselves. Even though they were getting killed."

"I still don't get it."

"Just what I said," he answers. "The kill rates, out of what should have been the volume of shots taken, the distance from the enemy, all of that — they were really low. Don't get me wrong, there was plenty of carnage, but a lot of it was due to cannon fire, and stupid shit like smoke inhalation and getting trampled. Hell, more died of disease and untreated wounds than were killed on the battlefield."

"They didn't want to kill anybody?" I repeat, knowing I sound stupid, but I just woke up and he's been awake all night thinking about this stuff, so I'm hoping he'll cut me some slack.

"I guess not," he says, shaking his head. "They estimate that only one in five, on both sides, would fire their weapons in battle. Or at least would fire directly at the enemy. Some just aimed high so they were sure to miss. The others pretended to fire, like I said. And they found the same thing in World War II. The same thing in all the wars. If it hadn't been for air and artillery — and finally the invention of automatic weapons — war back then would have been a big game of touch football."

"What about you guys?" I ask. "What about now?"

He stares deep into the valley, or seems to, maybe trying to see all the way through the thick fog blanketing the two rivers. From where we are, it looks as if the railroad bridge over the Potomac is sitting on clouds.

"We're good killers now," he says. "Better weapons. Better training. They got their shit together in Vietnam, got the firing rate up, way up. You might not want to kill — it's not in most people's nature — but they can, by god, train it into you. Unless you're a psychopath who just naturally loves it."

"Did they train it into you?" I ask, already knowing the answer.

He doesn't say. I guess he doesn't have to.

"But you believe in it, right?" I ask. "You believe in what you were doing over there. What you had to do." I don't want it to be a question, but of course it is.

"No," he says. "Maybe at first, but no. Every time you think you're doing something good for somebody, you end up hurting somebody else."

He presses into his leg yet again, only this time he doesn't wince.

"One thing we're damn good at is hurting people," he says. "But once we're done doling out all that hurt, we leave. No matter how many of our guys get blown away, get strung up or tortured or ambushed. Eventually we leave. But they're still there. They'll always be there. And our getting involved in the first place just stirs up mud and shit from the bottom, leaving the place worse than when we found it. Leaving us worse, too."

The fog is lifting now, quicker than I thought. I can see the river emerging from underneath. The low sun is on our faces.

"I can't believe that," I say. "It has to mean something, all you did over there. All your men did. All that sacrifice and everything."

Jeremy laughs a humorless laugh. "The truth is, it doesn't make a goddamn difference. But when you're over there, none of that matters — the pointlessness of it. You're trained to be a warrior, and so you become a warrior. And the bitch of it is that once you're back home, that damn pointless war is the only thing that *does* matter — not your job, not your wife and kids, not some stupid rock where Thomas Jefferson once took a leak."

"What about me?" I ask, before I can catch myself. It's a little-kid question. But he answers it.

"You're my brother," he says. "You're different."

But he doesn't explain any further.

"You know that night you picked me up at the sheriff's?" he asks.

I nod.

"When I got to Quantico, back on base, I couldn't get out. I just sat there in my truck for a couple of hours."

"How come?"

"I couldn't be around them anymore."

"'Them' who?"

"Marines," he says. "That's what finally broke it, got me ordered to have a psych eval: sitting in my truck when I should have been training my men. Not that there wasn't plenty of shit I'd done before that. But in the Corps, they only see shit like that when they absolutely can't ignore it anymore."

"Shit like what?" I ask, confused.

Jeremy is silent for the next several minutes, busying himself breaking down the M16, laying all the pieces carefully out on the tarp, cleaning them, then reassembling the gun, never taking his eyes off the view of the rivers, which are clear now, no trace of fog. "I couldn't be around any other Marines, not anybody in uniform. Because it hit me, sitting there, hiding in my fucking truck — the truck I twice already that week forgot to turn off and left running until it ran out of gas. But, yeah, it hit me right then and there, looking at them going into the building — I knew they would end up getting sent over there, and I just felt this thing in me, this, I don't know, this responsibility, that I had to be there, too, to not let anything happen to them. It was all on me to be there, to keep them alive, to bring them home safe. Only I couldn't, and I knew I couldn't."

He starts rubbing his left arm, hard, as if trying to erase the tattoos I know are hidden there under his sleeves: Marine Corps insignia, "Semper fi," and several sets of initials.

"What's with all the initials?" I ask quietly. I never had the nerve to ask before, and I wonder if I really want to know the answer.

"My men. My friends. The ones who didn't come back. The ones I didn't save."

"What about on the other arm?" I ask. I know he has more initials tattooed there.

He keeps rubbing his left arm. "They're the ones who got home alive," he says. "Only they brought too much of the damn war back with them."

He stops rubbing his arm. He snaps the ammo clip back into the M16, stands up, and fires off a round at the rising sun.

34

Jeremy is silent while I pack our gear, but since he's opened up, I don't want to let him just close back off again.

"Don't you think it might help?" I say. "Letting them do that evaluation, and just seeing what they come up with? Maybe they could figure out what might help with things."

He holds the M16 upright and taps his forehead on the barrel. "No."

"There're all kinds of things they could try," I say. "Medications and therapists, stuff like that. I'm sure something would work."

Jeremy pushes himself up to standing and shoulders the gun. "They don't order you to psych eval to find a way to fix you."

"Well, why, then?" I ask.

He sighs. "You dumb shit. They send you to psych eval because they've decided you're too fucked up to stay in the Corps."

Then he limps past me and starts the descent from Jefferson Rock.

I don't know whether to believe this or not. They sent Jeremy over for three tours of duty, they trained him and they promoted him, they trusted him to lead men into battle, and he nearly got killed doing it. They wouldn't just throw him away like that.

As slow as he's going, it doesn't take me long at all to catch up.

"Well, so what?" I ask. "You did your duty. You don't need to be in the Corps anymore."

"Forget it," he says.

And just like that, I feel Jeremy slipping away from me again. "Why'd you bring me along anyway?" I ask. "If you just wanted to be alone, to disappear, why'd you come by the game to get me?"

"Didn't," he says.

"Didn't what?"

"Didn't come to the game to get you." He doesn't turn around as he talks. I'm not sure how he's still standing, much less managing the steep incline. He's practically dragging his bad leg, and the blood has seeped all the way through his jeans again. "I just wanted to watch for a while, forget about some stuff. But then I saw you make a spectacular fool of yourself out on the field, and I figured you might need to get away as bad as I did."

"What stuff?" I ask. "What were you trying to forget?"

He stops, leans against a tree for a minute, then reshoulders the M16 and leads the way on past the church. I glance around to see if there's anyone up at this hour who might get the wrong idea, seeing a limping, bleeding, dirty vet carrying an automatic weapon out in the open like this. Luckily, the streets are empty.

"I went to Walter Reed," he says. "The medical center. Went to see Private First Class Atwell."

"From the video?" I ask, though how many Private First Class Atwells could there be.

"Yeah," Jeremy says. "That little ass wipe."

"How's he doing?" I ask.

Jeremy is sweating, even though it's chilly and still early morning. He wipes his face on his sleeve, then stares at the sleeve for a second, as if he's surprised to see that it's wet.

"About how you'd expect if you got half your face shot off," he says. "Can't hardly talk. Can't hardly see. They rebuilt his jaw and grafted butt skin over what's there now. Nose looks pretty good, though."

"What's going to happen to him?" We're walking again, Jeremy holding tight to the rail going down the steep stone stairs. I stay close behind in case he falls and I need to catch him, though he'd be pissed off if he knew.

"He'll be there for a while," Jeremy says. "They told me they have to do a couple more surgeries." He shakes his head, hard. "I should have made him keep down in that goddamn firefight. Dumb shit didn't know what he was doing out there."

"You saved his life," I remind him. "That's huge. Not very many people can say they did that."

"Didn't save enough of his life," Jeremy says. "Definitely not enough of his face. Don't know what's going to happen to him when he gets out. The kid doesn't have anywhere to go. No family, or none that wants him. His fucking girlfriend, she came to visit him once, got a good look at him, and he hasn't seen or heard from her since."

"That's terrible. He's got no other family?"

Jeremy shakes his head. "Nah. He was raised by his grandma, but she died when he was in high school. It's why he signed up. Poor bastard."

"You know, if you really want to help Atwell," I say, "you could get that psych eval and get better. And then help him yourself."

Jeremy stops at the bottom of the stone stairs, on Church Street, and looks back up at me. He looks like he's about ten years older than he was yesterday, his face drawn and sallow, sweat pouring off his forehead.

"You about done?" he says.

It's not a question.

Five minutes later, we're back on the shore by the canoe, waiting for water to boil on the little cookstove Jeremy bought. Sitting in the sand, neither of us talking now, looking out over the confluence of the rivers, serenaded by the rumbling sound of the Staircase Rapids upstream on the Shenandoah and some distant white water downstream on the Potomac. I argued for going into town and buying coffee, but Jeremy doesn't want to be around people. Plus he has another bottle of whiskey he must have stashed away last night that he retrieves and starts drinking way too fast.

"You should slow down on that," I say.

"You want some?" he asks, though he doesn't offer me the bottle.

I shake my head.

"Breakfast of champions," he says, and drinks more. Then he gets quiet for a while, back to staring at the slow boiling water.

"You want me to call River Riders?" I ask, finally interrupting the silence. "You said we'd call once we got here and have them come get us."

"Yeah, about that," Jeremy says, dumping coffee grounds into the water. He's about to say something else, when we hear a car pull up in the parking lot. A car door opens but doesn't close right away. There's the squawk of a radio — a police radio, I'm guessing.

Gravel crunches under boots on the path down to the river. We see him before he sees us — a young West Virginia sheriff's deputy. He looks like Barney Fife.

Jeremy does the friendly thing and calls out to him. "Want some coffee? Just brewing some up." He's slurring his words.

The deputy does a double take, as if we jumped out of hiding instead of just sitting here the whole time.

Jeremy lifts the coffeepot. "Gonna need your own cup, though. We only have the one."

He lays a cloth over our cup and pours.

The deputy steps closer but keeps a little distance from us. "Morning," he says, hands on his gun belt. He hooks a thumb through the dangling handcuffs. "Y'all spend the night here?"

"No," Jeremy says. "Just left the canoe here. What can we do for you?"

"Looking for two guys," the deputy says, fidgeting with his gear. "Just have a few questions we need to ask. Had kind of a problem up the river there yesterday."

"What sort of problem?" Jeremy asks, his speech slurring a little. He takes a drink of the nasty coffee, actually winces, then hands it to me.

"Got a fellow up that way, said he got beat on by a couple of guys. Said they took his girlfriend's truck. Already found the truck." He studies us for a minute. "That wouldn't have been you two boys, would it?"

"No," I say.

"Yes," Jeremy says.

I can't believe he just said that! I stare at him, waiting for him to explain to Barney Fife what happened, how Danny attacked Jeremy, and then Glory tried to attack him, too, and *did* attack me. And how we hadn't stolen the truck, just sort of rented it.

"Gonna need you to come with me, then," the deputy says. "There's questions that we're gonna need to ask you, like I said." He looks at Jeremy, then me, then Jeremy again. "Both of you."

Jeremy takes the coffee back. I haven't had but a sip. It burned my tongue. "I don't see that happening," he says, sounding drunk. "We're busy. Plus we paid the guy." I hope he doesn't get belligerent. I hope the deputy doesn't do anything that might set Jeremy off.

The deputy still fidgets nervously. "It's just to talk," he says. "Won't take long. Get this thing straightened out. You know how it is. Just have to follow up when there's a report. You can be back in your boat before you know it."

Jeremy starts to say something else but changes his mind. He stands, sways, nearly loses his balance, then takes a step toward the deputy. The deputy backs up. Jeremy shows his hands, which are empty, though I can see the outline of the 9mm tucked in the holster on his belt, under his shirt.

"I'll go with you," Jeremy says, nodding up the path to the parking lot. "But leave my little brother out of it. He didn't have anything to do with anything."

He doesn't wait for an answer — he isn't really asking anyway — just limps past the deputy and up the path.

The deputy looks at me. "You wait right here," he says.

They disappear up the path. I stay behind but strain to hear any of their conversation. They must have gone all the way up to the parking lot, though, because the only sounds I hear are the rivers and, after a few minutes, a train rumbling past through Harpers Ferry and on the railroad bridge overhead. Some early-morning hikers are up there on the pedestrian bridge. I see them when I turn to watch the train go over the Potomac. A little girl waves. Her mom takes her arm and hurries her away.

I don't know what else to do, so I walk slowly up the path after Jeremy and the deputy. Before I get to the parking lot, I hear the deputy's car start up, and by the time I get there, it's driving away. I yell after them and sprint after the car, but it doesn't stop. "Jeremy!"

They take a left out of the parking lot and disappear down the road that parallels the Shenandoah. I stop running and just stand there in the middle of the street, angry that I let Jeremy go off like that — without me.

But there's something else, too, and it takes a minute before it hits me.

That wasn't my brother I saw in the backseat of the cruiser.

It was the deputy.

35

I pace up and down the beach for the next twenty minutes, trying to figure out what I should do. The sun is fully out, and I feel exposed. I pull out my phone to call Annie but hang up before she answers, because how can I explain to anybody what just happened? I don't quite believe it myself. When she calls back, I let it go to voice mail. We've fallen down the rabbit hole and we're still falling, only Jeremy's off falling somewhere else, driving the deputy's car with the deputy in the back — but where? I keep nervously checking the path up to the parking lot and wondering if I should go somewhere, do something, but I don't have any answers.

More time passes. Half an hour. Maybe an hour.

More people go by on the footbridge overhead. Somebody throws a paper cup and it nearly hits me. Cold coffee splashes on my leg. Whoever did it is lost in a knot of people. Auto traffic picks up on the other bridge over the Potomac.

Jeremy shows up suddenly, dragging his bad leg even worse than before.

"Where have you been?" I demand. "What did you do to that deputy?"

"I took care of things," he says, no longer slurring his words. He's sweating profusely; maybe he got the whiskey out of his system that way. Or maybe he wasn't really as drunk as he seemed.

He busies himself throwing gear into the canoe, though it's still high up on the beach.

I follow him but refuse to help. "Took care of what? He was in the backseat. I saw him! You were driving his *cruiser.* What the hell's going on, Jeremy?"

He looks up at me. "I told you to stay down here."

"Well, I didn't," I say. "I went up there to see if you were OK. How did he end up in the back?"

Jeremy turns to the canoe. "We had different ideas about what should happen," he says. "I didn't like the way the conversation was going, and I definitely didn't like it when he decided to pull his weapon. So I took care of it."

"You disarmed him? You took his gun away? Oh my god!" I can't believe this. I can't believe any of it. We're in

210

so much trouble now — so much more than anything like getting kicked off a football team or being suspended from school. "Where is he now? What did you do with him?"

"You need to just calm the hell down, Shane. I took him somewhere and left him to cool off. That's all. I'm sure they'll find him soon enough. They have GPS."

"Where is he?" I ask again, getting pissed.

"He's sitting in the backseat of his car. Locked in. I left the windows open in the front seat. I made sure to lock his gun belt in the glove compartment so that no one could come by and take it. I figured that would get him into some pretty serious trouble. Anyway, worst thing that's going to happen to him is he'll get a little thirsty and a little bored."

"This is crazy," I say. "Totally, totally, bullshit crazy. Why did you do it?"

He shrugs his usual shrug. "I didn't feel like going with him."

"They were just going to ask us some questions," I say. "We could have explained everything."

"Maybe," he says. "Maybe not. Anyway, it's done."

Jeremy finishes stuffing our gear into the canoe. He carefully wraps the M16 in the tarp and sets it in the back within quick reach of where he sits and steers.

Then he looks up at me again. "I've gotta go," he says.

"Where are we going now?" I ask.

"*We?*" he says. "Nowhere. You're staying here. I already told the little deputy you didn't have anything to do with anything. You just call somebody. Call Mom or the Colonel.

Go wait in town somewhere, maybe with that girl you like. They'll come pick you up."

"But what about you?" I ask, panicking.

"Thought I'd keep paddling for a while," he says.

"But there's nowhere to go, Jeremy," I say. "They'll catch us. They know who we are and everything."

"You're staying here," Jeremy says. "I already told you. I'm doing this last leg by myself."

"What the hell are you talking about?" I snap. "Last leg to where?"

"Jesus, Shane," he says. "You really need to learn some goddamn geography. This is the Potomac." He points to the wide river in front of us. "It runs back into Virginia. You've crossed it a million times — every trip you ever made into Washington."

"So you're going to Washington?"

"No," he says. "Only to Great Falls."

"You can't canoe down Great Falls," I say, as if he doesn't already know that. As if everybody in the world doesn't know that. Of course I've been to Great Falls before, and of course I know that it's on the Potomac, and of course I know that the Potomac continues on, once it crashes over the falls, to DC and into the Chesapeake Bay and the Atlantic Ocean. But that isn't what I meant at all when I asked him, "Last leg to where?"

He collects the paddles and throws them in the boat.

"Great Falls is where people in kayaks go to drown," I

say, picturing the raging storm of cataracts there, which I've seen a couple of times from the observation posts at Great Falls Park.

"Well, fortunately I'm not in a kayak," Jeremy says, his voice so heavy with sarcasm that for a second he sounds like the Colonel. Then his voice softens. A little. "Anyway, I'll pull off somewhere along the way. Don't worry."

He drags the canoe down the beach and over rocks to the river's edge, not seeming to care that the jagged edges of the stones scrape long gashes into the fiberglass.

I step over to help him, though I'm not sure why. He doesn't want me with him anymore — if he ever wanted me with him in the first place — and I'm in enough trouble as it is. I came on this trip to get away after totally embarrassing myself in front of everybody. I stayed to help Jeremy. But now — Jesus — the last thing I want to do is get back in the canoe and back on the river. Paddling farther is just delaying the inevitable, probably making it even worse. And there are going to be all kinds of charges for what Jeremy just did to that deputy: assault with a deadly weapon, kidnapping, who knows what else? And I'm the accomplice. This is the stuff they send you to jail for — and for a long time.

Jeremy climbs in the back of the canoe and sits, his end of the boat in the water. "Push me off," he says. "Then wait an hour. Then go call somebody."

I do what Jeremy says — the first part anyway. But instead of letting him loose in the current by himself, I jump in and grab my paddle. We've come this far together, and whatever happens, I can't abandon Jeremy now.

Jeremy curses at me for the next hour as we paddle down the river, the Potomac rushing fast and hard, probably from heavy rains up in the West Virginia mountains. A wall of rock rises above us to the north, a low bluff to the south. A mile downriver we shoot under a bridge, and I can see from the traffic that it's full-on morning now, and Jeremy is *still* letting me have it for getting in the canoe.

I just paddle harder, doing my best to tune him out, doing my best to tune out all the voices in my head, that loud chorus telling me how much trouble I'm in — how totally fucked Jeremy and I both are.

Jeremy finally shuts up and turns his attention to paddling, too, and now we're flying down the river. I don't know where I'm getting the strength to do this, and I definitely don't know where he's getting his, but we power on, matching each other stroke for stroke for the next hour, and another hour after that, until my arms and shoulders and back and neck are screaming in pain, but even then I don't let myself stop, and Jeremy doesn't stop either, we just keep up this pace as if we might be able to outrun everything that's behind us — everything that's behind Jeremy: the law, Annie and the kids, Unauthorized Absence, the wars, ghosts.

Tears pour from my eyes and snot leaks down my face, but I don't pause even a second to wipe any of it away. All those hours in the weight room, on the practice field, on the track, running stadium steps, all that grinding—it's prepared me for this, for paddling through bullshit pain. If Jeremy can do it, I can do it, and wherever he's going, I'm going, too. I'm all in.

We paddle until I'm delirious, blind to everything except the motion of dragging my paddle through the water, right side, left side. Jeremy breaks his stroke only to steer us around rocks that appear suddenly, that I often don't notice until we're just barely skirting them safely or scraping around them. We're in racing flat water until we're suddenly in rapids and just as suddenly back in flat water. I'm vaguely aware of people on the bank, then no people, just trees. We go under another bridge, around long islands that split the river in two. I don't stop crying—silently: I won't let Jeremy know, no matter what. I just keep digging, digging, digging, sweat pouring down my face until I don't have any more sweat. I'm so thirsty that I let my jaw drop, keep my mouth open so I'll at least get some hint of moisture off the river, some spray from the rapids. My tongue feels too swollen for me to bring my lips together anyway. We race on.

And then we stop. Or Jeremy stops. Without a word he steers us to one of the islands, and without a word I stand up, stagger out of the canoe, and on shaky legs pull us up on a narrow spit of sandy beach. I'm not about to let go, though—not until Jeremy gets out—because I'm afraid if I let my guard down, he'll shove back off into the river without me.

"Here," he says, tossing me a T-shirt he fishes out of our gear. "Clean yourself up already." There's half a bottle of water — I think it's our last — and he hands it to me and tells me to drink. I worry that if I take more than a sip, I won't be able to stop and I'll gulp it all down and there won't be any for him, so I wet my lips and my tongue and then hand it back because he must be parched, too, and he's the reason I'm here.

He tries to hand the water back, but I refuse. Jeremy's will is always stronger than anybody else's, though, and when he says he'll only drink more if I do first, I cave and drink, and then collapse on the ground, staring up at the green canopy and the diamonds of light filtering through. I close my eyes and they burn. Everything burns.

36

After a few minutes Jeremy kicks me. "Come on, ass wipe,"
he says. "Help me hide the canoe."

It's not lost on me that it's what he calls Private Atwell, too.

I get up, and we drag the canoe into a thick stand of trees
and brush. "This'll do," he says. I drop my end and collapse
again, spread-eagle, on the rough ground. He winces as he
lets himself down as well, but he doesn't sprawl on his back
like me. He pulls out the tarp and busies himself once again
cleaning the M16.

"You going to just shoot the next cop that comes along?"
I ask.

"Didn't shoot the last one," he says.

"That must have taken a lot of restraint," I say.

Jeremy lets that one go.

We go back to not talking, just like in the past couple of hours of hard paddling. I have a hundred questions, but he only answers things when he feels like it, so what's the use of pushing anything?

"Your phone still working?" Jeremy asks when he finishes with the M16.

I'd fallen asleep — god knows how, with everything going on. I fish the phone out of my pocket and turn it on, surprised to see that there's reception here. I hesitate before handing it over. "Don't throw it into the river, OK?"

He grunts as he pushes himself to a standing position, and drags himself away, deeper onto the island. I hear him wading through the brush, the sound getting fainter over the next couple of minutes. I don't know how wide this island is. I wish I'd checked for messages before giving him the phone.

He left the M16 sitting on the tarp — all cleaned and loaded and ready to fire. I pick it up and sight down the barrel at a tree trunk. I think about going back down to the river and throwing the damn thing in. Maybe sneaking up on Jeremy, grabbing the 9mm, and throwing that away, too.

But I don't have the guts to do anything like that, which obviously he knows or he wouldn't have left the M16 behind.

Maybe Annie will be able to talk some sense into him — I assume that's who he's calling — talk him into ending this crazy trip we're on and turn himself in to the police. Maybe since he's a veteran, and he's been through so much, and he's supposed to be getting a psych eval, and help — maybe they'll just let it all go: beating up that redneck at the dam and taking the truck; kidnapping the deputy. My heart sinks as I think about everything he's done. Even as hopeful as I'm trying to be, I know there's no way he gets out of jail free for all that.

I'm still standing by the river, still holding the M16, when he comes up behind me. The Potomac is raging past even faster than when we left Harpers Ferry.

"Seen anybody?" he asks.

"No," I say. "You mean like the police?"

"I mean like anybody: boats on the river. Anything in the air. Anybody on shore."

"There's not really a place over there to get down to the shore," I point out. "That bluff's too steep."

"You'd be surprised at what somebody can climb up or down," he says.

I offer him the M16. "I was thinking about tossing it in the river," I say.

He takes it. "Now why in the hell would you do something like that?"

"Because it scares me," I say. "All of it scares me, Jeremy."

"I know," he says, suddenly serious. "Sorry to drag you into this."

I don't respond, because there's a sound from the river: a boat motor. We both see it as soon as we hear it — the bow of a police boat — and dive to the ground as it slowly passes. For a minute it seems to slow down even more, and I'm afraid it's going to come over to the island. It swings close and we hug the ground.

And then it's gone, cruising on down the river.

Jeremy sits up first. "Did you see if it was the Virginia or Maryland police? This side of the river is the Virginia side. Maryland is on the other side of the island."

I shake my head. "What difference does it make?"

He shrugs.

"So what now?" I ask.

Jeremy looks at his left hand, at where the missing finger is. "Hang out here until dark, then shove off. I checked the forecast on your phone. There'll be clear enough sky and enough moonlight tonight for us to make it to Great Falls by morning."

"And then?"

"And then we'll see."

"See what, exactly?"

He shrugs again. "There's a park on the Virginia side. One on the Maryland side, too, if you'd rather go there."

"Whatever," I say. "But we pull off the river at one of those parks and we turn ourselves in. Right?"

"Worth considering," he says, now smiling.

"Did you tell Annie all this?" I ask.

"Pretty much," he says. "She says hi, by the way."

He hasn't given me back my cell phone, and I ask for it

now. But he just shakes his head. "Don't have it anymore," he says.

I don't even get mad when he tells me this. Maybe I was expecting it. Or maybe I've given up having any sort of expectations when it comes to Jeremy and this never-ending journey we're on.

Jeremy's not even using his left leg anymore, just dragging it behind him when he walks. His pants are soaked in blood, but he won't let me look at his wound. We're out of bottled water, so there's no way I can clean it anyway, but at least I could change the gauze, wrap something tighter around it for some pressure, maybe stanch the bleeding — if he'd let me.

He settles back down on the tarp and leans against the canoe, cradling the M16. A dragonfly lands on the barrel and he tries to shake it off, but it won't budge. He blows on it, but it still doesn't move, so he lets it stay. It's an odd sight — Jeremy and his gun and his dragonfly. I'm sitting against a tree opposite him. It's surprisingly warm even in the deep shade of the trees, and I doze again, off and on. If Jeremy falls asleep, too, he must time it perfectly with when I've nodded off, because every time I wake up, he's still sitting there, eyes open, watchful, waiting.

37

Something startles me awake. A siren. A screeching bird. I don't know what. I sit bolt upright, my brain crusty from deep sleep. It takes me a second to realize I'm flailing around with my arms, and kicking at somebody who isn't there. I've got sand in my eyes, grit between my teeth. I spit and spit, desperate for water we don't have.

I rub my eyes and see nothing but red for a minute, and then as my vision clears I see Jeremy, slumped over.

I crawl over to him and pull him upright. "Jeremy!" I yell. "Jeremy!"

I panic, worried that he might be dead or dying. I feel for his pulse and — thank god — he has one. I press my hand on his chest and he's still breathing.

"Jeremy!" I call to him again, right into his ear. "Wake up! What's wrong?"

He stirs but doesn't open his eyes. I wonder if it's the blood loss. Or barely sleeping for the past week. Or sheer exhaustion. But he's a Marine captain! He can't collapse like this, no matter what.

I grab a couple of bottles and run down to the river to fill them. Even dirty water is better than none. He's still out when I get back. I pour some on his face and lift the bottle to his lips. And then he drinks. A lot. Pausing only to lick his dry, cracked lips. And then he drinks more. He doesn't stop until the bottle is empty. And then he looks at me.

"What's going on?" he asks, as if it's all been nothing.

It's late afternoon. I've been asleep. God knows how long he's been out.

"You fell asleep," I say. "Or passed out. I couldn't get you to wake up."

"Well, I'm awake now," he says. "Where'd you get the water?"

"River," I say.

He struggles to sit up taller. "Not sure that was such a good idea. You drink some, too?"

I shake my head.

He presses his hands against his temples. "Got anything for a headache?" he asks. "I'm guessing not."

I shake my head again. "You OK? I mean besides the headache? I couldn't wake you up," I repeat.

"Guess it was my turn to fall asleep on fire watch. I'm up now, though, so you can stop hyperventilating."

And that's the end of that.

"When do we shove off?" I ask, looking around, as if there's anything to see besides the same thick flora we've been hiding in since late morning.

"Dusk ought to do it," Jeremy says. "If anybody else is looking for us, they'll knock off by then."

"Think they are?" I ask. "Still looking for us, I mean?"

"Sure," he says. "Big game of hide-and-seek."

Now that I know he's OK, I'm back to wanting to yell at him — that this isn't some game, that it's our lives, and we're probably going to jail.

But I don't say any of that, of course, and an hour later, at dusk, we drag the canoe to the river and launch ourselves into the current.

The mountains are gone but not the heavily wooded shoreline. There's a road on the Maryland side, and headlights flash at times through the trees. I keep straining for signs of the police boat coming back our way, or hiding onshore, waiting for us. Meanwhile, every paddle stroke sends pain tearing from my shoulders down my back. My arms are leaden, almost too heavy to lift and too weak to grab much water when I pull, though the Potomac is still running so high and fast it probably doesn't much matter. Jeremy grunts behind me, and his breathing sounds ragged. I keep sneaking looks back but can't see much in the growing darkness.

The river keeps splitting in two, around more of these long islands. Jeremy usually stays on the Virginia side, to the right, but once when we go left, closer to the Maryland shore, we hit a stretch of rapids so wild we nearly lose the canoe. Every dark shape in front of me looks like a rock and I paddle furiously to keep us clear of them, but we keep banging into them anyway — glancing blows that send us shooting off nearly sideways before Jeremy can steer us straight again. I strain to see clear channels for us to shoot through and yell directions back to him as best I can, but it's all hit or miss. He curses constantly — at the river, at the rocks, at the darkness, at me.

Finally we break free of that wild stretch and paddle into flat water again. The water is still high and fast, though, and it feels as if we're flying down the river, even with my weak paddling, hurtling headlong toward Great Falls.

Deep into the night, after we've been in a stretch of flat water for a good hour, Jeremy asks me if I'm still awake.

"Yeah," I say back. "Who'd you think was paddling?"

"Could just be sleep-paddling," he says. "Doesn't look like you're doing much."

I splash water on him, then brace myself for getting splashed back, but nothing comes.

"I, uh, thought I should tell you — again," he says, fumbling for words, almost sounding drunk again, except I know he's all out of liquor. "That I'm sorry. Pretty sure I said it before, but maybe I just thought it. Anyway, I am. Sorry, I mean. For getting you into all this."

"It's OK," I answer, even though it's not. But what else can I say?

"Not that you should have disobeyed a direct fucking order to stay out of the canoe back at Harpers Ferry," he adds.

He doesn't say anything else for a while, and I go back to paddling — harder this time, as he steers us into the channel around another island, and then through a small stretch of rapids. We clunk hard into a couple of rocks, trees crowding the banks on both sides where this section of the Potomac narrows, blocking out the moonlight. Plus I'm distracted, because something tells me now is the time to ask him the question I've been avoiding the whole trip.

"Jeremy," I say. "I have to know something. And you have to tell me the truth."

There's a jolt as the canoe glances off another rock. "Watch it," he says. "And what's your question? I don't make any promises, though."

Ask him, ask him, ask him, I tell myself. Finally I do.

"Did you hit her?" I ask, my mouth so dry I can barely get the words out.

"Who?" he says, but he knows.

"Annie," I say. "She said it was an accident, that Nelly threw a toy at her. . . ."

I want him to say no, to get mad at me for even suggesting such a thing. I want him to yell at me, cuss me out for insulting him like that, for not having any trust in him, any faith.

We paddle for a long time before he answers, and even though I know what's coming — have known it all along, really, but especially because of how he hasn't answered right away — my heart still sinks when he says it.

"Yeah," he says. "Fuck. Yeah. I did."

And then — finally — Jeremy talks.

38

Jeremy's voice is ragged so it's hard to hear him over our paddles splashing in the river — over the dull roar in my head.

There are these rages, he says, these awful, crippling headaches and blind rages that come over him. Making him do things. He tells me he pulled a gun on a guy outside a bar once — the asshole had keyed Jeremy's truck — and he still doesn't know why he didn't shoot the son of a bitch. He tells me how much he liked killing those wild pigs, and especially the ones he shot up close to finish off. But then how disgusted he felt afterward, a too-familiar feeling of disgust that he's had since his first tour of duty. He talks about drinking, and how much he wishes he had a drink right now, and how he can't even remember the things he does sometimes and doesn't know if it's because he drank until he blacked out or if it's one of those fucking brain injuries they say he might have.

He says he got thrown one time when an IED detonated and tossed his Humvee across the road like it was nothing, and the door was ajar, so it didn't absorb the blast the way it was supposed to, and two men got killed.

He says he still has a loud ringing in his ears sometimes, and it gets so bad he can't think, can't sleep, and the only way to make it go away is to drink more and take pills.

And then, when the kids get too clingy or won't stop crying, or Annie says something that sets him off, or for reasons he can't begin to explain or understand himself, the rages come, and he has to get out of there before he does something he'll regret. He has to get in his truck and drive as fast as he can until the trees on the roadside blur into one solid wall and he's outrunning his headlights and the only thing keeping him from losing control around every blind curve is pure stupid luck.

Not that he thinks he has any more luck coming to him, he says — not good luck, definitely. All of that got used up in the wars, keeping him alive when guys around him didn't make it, or keeping him from having his face shot off when other guys lost theirs, like Private Atwell, that stupid fucking ass wipe who wouldn't keep his head down. But why'd

Atwell have to be the one to lose his face? It was Jeremy who couldn't keep all the men together when they came under fire earlier. If Jeremy had done his goddamn job, he wouldn't have had to go after Atwell, and Atwell would still have a goddamn face. . . .

I keep paddling, and we keep slamming into rapids and they keep bucking us around wildly, but somehow I don't miss one single word of what Jeremy is saying.

"I shouldn't have gone back to see her," he says. "I knew I wasn't in my right mind. But I'd been such a shit to her before I left for Quantico. I hated leaving things that way. I never thought I'd . . . Jesus."

His tone changes. "They want too goddamn much from me! I don't have it anymore. I don't have anything. Annie — she thinks she knows me. But she doesn't know me. Not anymore. I'm not that guy. That guy is dead. That guy she married. He's done. He's fucking done."

I'm still paddling, still listening hard, taking it all in but saying nothing, just letting Jeremy's confession or whatever it is roll out over the black water, drift off through the deepening night. We run into more rocks, scrape ourselves past, but he doesn't bother to chastise me anymore.

Jeremy's sobbing now, saying how sorry he is, how goddamn sorry, and how he doesn't deserve forgiveness — not Annie's, not mine, not his men's, not anybody's — and if I wasn't so bone-tired, if my brain wasn't on overload, I would tell him that of course he deserves forgiveness — for everything he's done in the war, and for everything he's done since coming home, even for hitting Annie — but he has to get help, he can't keep running like this, waiting for his luck to dry up. He has to stop, this all has to stop!

But even if I could manage to speak, I wouldn't be able to say any of that, because the river isn't through with us yet.

In the middle of another stretch of rapids, the river slams us hard into another rock — so suddenly there's no time to react, no way to brace ourselves. Jeremy yells something as the canoe nearly flips. I throw myself to the other side to right it, but then the boat careens wildly that way and water pours inside, washing gear into the river. The canoe rocks back up. Jeremy jumps to save the tarp-wrapped M16, but it gets away from him and disappears into the water.

We keep sloshing back and forth, the boat twisting, now sideways, now going backward, slamming into more rocks, and we're fighting to stay upright, sinking lower as we take on more water. I clutch my paddle between my knees and bail as hard as I can with both hands. And finally, I don't even know how, we're turned back around and facing downstream and out of the rough water.

The canoe is steady now, though still riding low, and I'm still bailing furiously in case we hit more rapids, more white water that will wash into the boat if we don't get more clearance. Jeremy isn't helping, though. He slams his paddle against the side of the boat, still cursing about the M16.

"You still have the 9mm," I say.

He pulls it out of the holster and checks it, then puts it away and holds his paddle the same way he always held the M16. He sits there like that for the next several minutes, gripping the paddle so tightly that I'm afraid he'll break it in half.

39

The roaring begins at dawn. Or rather, we're close enough to hear it, finally, at dawn, as we draw near to the giant cataract that is Great Falls. Jeremy's guidebook is long gone, but clearly he read ahead. He tells me we're skirting Conn Island and the river widens here, deceptively flat but still fast. There's a dam just up ahead, he says, a several-foot drop. The river narrows after that, and keeps dropping — forty feet in less than a tenth of a mile, the river broken into a dozen foaming channels that crash around boulders turned slick and black from fast water, until the biggest drop of all, through a narrow chute and twenty feet down into a churning pool that holds everything under — log, animal, kayaker — only releasing it another mile downriver, or never, held under by rocks, fallen trees, complicated underwater currents and whirlpools and eddies. If you surface, you come up in Mather Gorge, a twisting, raging stretch of river between Great Falls cliffs and flat-topped bedrock islands, with sides so sheer they might as well be Mount Everests for all the good they'll do you if you're being sucked down the river.

But we're getting out before any of that. Jeremy points to shore, to the park on the Virginia side, just before the dam.

Neither of us is paddling anymore. It hardly matters, the current is so strong. I'm so tired, so far past tired, that I doubt I can do it anyway. Jeremy steers us. That's about it.

It's a bloodred sunrise. I try to say reassuring things to my brother: "It'll be all right. We'll explain. They'll take into consideration who you are and what you've been through. Everybody is going to stand by you. All of us. Me, Mom, Annie.

"I'll find a phone and call Annie once we pull off the river," I say. "Or Mom. They'll come get us. We'll do that first. We'll go home. We'll turn ourselves in from there or whatever. Or maybe you could go straight to the psych eval. Hell, I don't know, Jeremy. But we'll figure it out. I promise."

I know I have no business making any promises, but I have to say something to try to lift Jeremy's spirits.

I look back at him, but he doesn't meet my gaze. He looks terrible. I'm sure we both do, but him especially. I

realize he's steeling himself through all the pain he's in just to get us off the river.

I hop out of the canoe to pull us up halfway out of the river, enough so the current won't take the boat once we both get out. Jeremy just sits there.

"You OK?" I ask.

He shakes his head. "Don't think I can walk," he says. "Leg's gone numb. Don't think I can put any weight on it."

"Maybe it's just from sitting so long," I say. "Maybe it just stiffened up, and moving around will help."

He lays down his paddle in the canoe, grips the sides, and forces himself to stand. As soon as he takes a step on his bad leg, he collapses. He doesn't say anything, doesn't make a sound, just goes down.

"Why don't you go on ahead," he says. "There's gotta be a phone up there somewhere in the park."

I look up the sloping hill, but all I see are weeds and brush and trees. "What park?" I ask.

"It's up there," he says. "It was on the map. Just cut through there and you'll come to it."

"I'm not leaving you here," I say. "Let me at least get you out of the canoe."

He agrees to that, and I practically have to lift Jeremy and carry him to a spot onshore. As exhausted as I am, he feels light to me. There's blood on my arm when I stand back up. From his leg.

"This is bad," I say, but he just gives me this impassive look.

"It is what it is," he says.

"I'll go," I say. "But you have to swear you'll stay right here."

He grimaces. "Where the hell else am I going to go?"

I look out at the river, downstream. There's a white line cutting diagonally across the full width of the Potomac, passing the head of the island, visible now in the growing light of morning. It's where the river flows over the last dam before the Falls. The point of no return.

"I'll be here when you get back," Jeremy says, and I go.

It's not much of a park. I cross a path that must follow the river, then a mostly cleared area leading up to a parking lot. I step out from under tree cover and into the empty gravel lot and look around. There's a concrete-block restroom on the other side, but nothing else. No phone anywhere.

I'm just standing, wondering what to do next, when a car drives up, crunching gravel and spitting out rocks from under the tires. It's a Virginia Highway Patrol car, followed by a couple of sheriff's cruisers. They must not see me right away because they pull slowly into the lot and circle, and seem as if they're about to leave. I keep standing where I am, frozen, hoping they won't notice me, hoping I'm somehow invisible in the gray morning light, but then the Highway Patrol car's brakes flash on, and the others' as well, and they stop.

Officers and deputies jump out of the vehicles, and one shouts at me, "Stay right there!" and at first I do, but only for

a second, only until they take a couple of steps in my direction, and then I turn and run, flying down the hill back to the river, to warn Jeremy, to prepare him, I'm not sure for what. I just know that I have to tell him that we're already caught, that I won't be able to get us home first to Annie and Mom.

They're running after me, yelling at me to stop, but I keep going, though my tired legs threaten to buckle under me. One of the officers yells my name—"Shane Dupree!"— and I don't know how they know it's me and not Jeremy, or just some guy who happened to be there, but I guess if you're looking for somebody and see somebody and that somebody runs off, you just naturally think it's who you're after.

"Jeremy!" I yell as I'm nearing the river. "Jeremy!"

I burst through the brush and run back down to the narrow beach and the canoe and him, only he's not there, and the canoe's not there either. I skid to a stop in the sand. "Jeremy!"

I look frantically up and down the beach, and then I see him—back out on the river, paddling alone toward the tip of Conn Island and toward the Maryland side, toward the dam.

I hear the police storming through the brush behind me, and there's no time to think this through, to think about anything, I just kick my boots off and dive into the river and start swimming after Jeremy. The shock of the cold takes my breath away, so I can't shout anymore at first, and my jeans are already dragging me down, despite the rush of adrenaline that has me slicing through the water, but wherever he thinks he's going, he's not going there without me.

I keep trying to yell out to Jeremy, and finally he hears me. He looks around and sees me swimming after him. "What the fuck, Shane?" he shouts, and he turns the canoe and paddles upriver to get me, while the officers back onshore are screaming their heads off for us to get off the river, get off the river, get off the fucking river! It's pulling us — me, Jeremy, the canoe — closer and closer to the dam.

He gets to me and reaches out and grabs my arm, which is a good thing, because my strength has about given out, but neither of us has enough left to get me inside the canoe. It tilts hard to one side, and I realize we're going over the dam if we don't do something, so I scream at Jeremy to just let me go and to paddle for the island, maybe he can still make it, but he won't let go, and then there's no time to make a decision because the river makes it for us, sweeping us over the dam and dropping us several feet into the water below, the canoe going one way, me and Jeremy — him still gripping my arm somehow — going the other.

But that's just the beginning, because the river narrows so much here that the current picks up speed and we're back on the roller coaster.

"Turn!" Jeremy screams at me over the roar of the waves, the river slicing around enormous boulders. "Feet first! Push off the rocks!"

Somehow I manage to turn just in time and avoid slamming headfirst into a boulder, but there's another boulder after that, and another, and Jeremy and I are pinballing down the raging river, doing our best to avoid cracking our heads open. I'm not able to get into position in time at one point and I jam my shoulder hard into a boulder and can't feel Jeremy's hand on my arm anymore and I'm underwater for a second and then back to the surface but he's not too far away and I push off another boulder with my feet and try to force myself close enough to grab him but now he goes under and I dive after him as best I can and flail in the water blind and my fingers graze something and it's him so I grab hold and come back up, dragging him up with me, and we hit another rock and another after that, battered back and forth and getting sucked farther and farther down the river by the fierce and relentless current, racing toward the Falls.

I can't tell if Jeremy's even conscious anymore. His eyes are open but he doesn't seem to be seeing me or doing anything at this point to protect himself, so I pull him behind me, trying to keep his head out of the water as we career from boulder to boulder, doing the best I can to absorb the blows, but also trying to grab on to one of them, too, or a log or any handhold, to stop us from being flung over the Falls, which are now less than ten feet away.

Finally, miraculously, I get enough of my body lined up so that when I slam into one low boulder, I'm able to slip my hand into a crevice and drag myself halfway up onto the rock, pulling Jeremy behind me, who comes out of his stupor or whatever and grabs the rock with one hand and clutches me with the other. But the river grabs us, too, and pulls with a force that I know we can't hold out against for very long, and I curse at it, like it's something evil out to kill us, out to rip Jeremy out of my grip and me out of his.

My hands are cramping and I can feel myself slipping, feel the end to all this — to everything — coming any second. My face is inches away from Jeremy's and we're yelling at each other over the din of the Falls, which is now only a body's length away — though I don't even know what either of us is yelling, maybe just "Hold on! Hold on! Hold on!"

I look up for a second and am surprised by what I see: a bright sky, no clouds, just all this brilliant blue and sunshine, and somehow I hear what he's saying to me, and I realize he's smiling — actually smiling!

"It's OK, Shane." That's what he's saying, which is crazy, totally crazy. "You'll be OK."

And he lets go of the rock and uses his free hand to try to force me to release my grip on his arm. But I won't do it. I hold on tighter.

"I've got you, goddamnit!" I say. "Just stay with me, Jeremy!"

He just shakes his head, though, as if this is all just a whole lot of nothing and not our lives.

He says, "You hang on — as long as it takes, you hear?" He looks into my eyes, and I want to scream at him, "No no no no no!" but that look . . . that look . . .

He forces my fingers off his arm. "Semper fi," he says.

And then he's swept away over the Falls and gone.

Nine Months Later

I still think about Jeremy all the time, replaying our trip down the river over and over in my head, all the decisions that weren't really decisions — or not conscious ones anyway. What if I hadn't yelled out to him when I was running from the police? What if we hadn't pulled up alongside Glory and Danny and the police had never been after us in the first place? What if I had been able to hold on tighter, to Jeremy and to the rock? What if I hadn't been so stupid — thinking I could fix him — and refused to go on that crazy trip to begin with?

I know some people think what happened was intentional — that Jeremy never planned on coming back. But they're wrong. He had a gun and could have used it anytime if that was true. And he wouldn't have put me through anything like what happened at Great Falls. Not on purpose.

Plus they weren't there to see him when he tore my fingers off his arm. They didn't see the look in his eyes, the one that said he knew his luck had run out, and he was sorry, but it was his job to get his men home alive — to get me home alive — no matter what.

They didn't find his body for three days, miles downstream. Annie drove up to identify him at a hospital in Fairfax, in their basement morgue. She probably didn't have to; he still had his dog tags on, a Marine to the end. She told me he looked peaceful. I'm not sure I believe her, but if it was a lie, it was a nice lie, and just like her to say something like that to make me feel not so bad.

West Virginia wanted me back to face charges for something — I'm still not sure what — but Virginia wouldn't send me. They said I'd been through enough and for me to just stay out of West Virginia for a while. They didn't say how long, but it doesn't matter, since I'm never going back there anyway.

I only ended up missing a couple of weeks of school in the end, which surprised me. It felt like a lifetime. Coach even asked me to come back on the team, in time for the playoffs. I thanked him but said no — my heart wasn't in it anymore.

Mom goes up to Arlington a lot to visit Jeremy's grave at the National Cemetery. The Colonel drives up with her. She says he feels responsible for what happened, which is something I don't get. Maybe he means it was his fault because if he hadn't made Jeremy join the Marines in the first place, Jeremy would still be alive. But that's stupid, because no matter how he ended up there, Jeremy loved the Corps.

I've been up to Arlington a couple of times, too. Once I even drove up with Hannah, which should have been weird but wasn't. We sat next to Jeremy for a long time, not saying much but not really needing to. It was enough just getting to be close.

We aren't dating or anything. Just hanging out. Hannah says she doesn't want to be one of those girls who try to rescue a guy who's in need or whatever. I told her I don't need rescuing, but she just smiled and said, "Let's just see."

Annie took what happened the hardest of anyone. She held herself together as long as she could — through the funeral and for a couple of months after. I kept going by as much as I could, but I had a feeling that my being there was hard for her. Maybe it reminded her too much of Jeremy whenever she saw me. Maybe seeing me made her think about all her own questions about what happened, which she'll probably always have no matter how many times she asks me and no matter how many times and how many ways I try to answer.

Eventually she told me her mom was coming up from Richmond to stay with her and help with the girls. She said I should start calling first before dropping by. I still go over some, but it's not like it used to be.

Private Atwell has been living with us for a month now, which is probably the biggest thing that's changed. It was Mom's idea to take him in after I told her about Jeremy visiting him at Walter Reed and about Tyler not having any family. The Colonel said no — at first — until Mom stared him straight in the face and said, "Either he comes here or I go where he is." Mom didn't look away until the Colonel caved, which, come to think of it, might be the biggest change of all.

They put Tyler in Jeremy's old bedroom. And I don't know how Mom managed it, but she got the Colonel to drive him to his appointments at the VA hospital down in Richmond. The Colonel gets on Tyler's ass if he isn't doing his physical therapy, but it's different from the way he used to get on Jeremy's ass, or even mine. And you can tell that Tyler even kind of likes it.

Tyler still has a long way to go with his PT and his surgeries. He's hard to understand at first, and his face takes some getting used to. But if you put in the effort, you can make out what he's saying. He's actually pretty funny, even though he might have to repeat himself a few times before you can understand his jokes.

He came into my bedroom late one night after he'd been

with us a couple of weeks. He wanted to give me something—
a plaque he'd helped the Colonel make with all of Jeremy's
medals mounted on it. They'd spent days huddled together
working on it out in the garage. He tried to speak but
couldn't get the words out, so he pressed his hand over his
heart, and then pressed his hand over my heart, too.

The other day we drove out to the mall in Jeremy's truck,
which is mine now. Annie didn't want it, and she said it
wasn't really practical for her and the kids anyway. Tyler and
I were stopped at that same light, and that same homeless
guy who stole our lawn mower was there.

I rolled down my window, and the homeless guy wandered over. "Sergeant Frank," I said, and he looked confused,
though I don't know if it was because he didn't recognize
me and didn't know how I knew his name or because Frank
wasn't actually his name.

I nodded over at Tyler in the passenger seat. "This
is Private First Class Tyler Atwell," I said. "Also from the
Two-Five."

Sergeant Frank stared at Tyler for a long time—long
enough that the light changed and people started honking—
and then he lifted his hand and gave a kind of salute, though
he might just have been shielding his eyes from the afternoon sun.

Tyler gave him five dollars, and I drove on through the
light and to the mall. We were going to buy shoes.

AUTHOR'S NOTE AND ACKNOWLEDGMENTS

I owe a considerable debt to my friend Chris Kerr for his Marine's-eye reading of the *Great Falls* manuscript and for helping me with some of the finer points of river navigation.

Roger Corbett's masterful *Virginia Whitewater: A Paddler's Guide to the Rivers of Virginia* was an essential source for me in writing *Great Falls*. Those familiar with the topography of the Shenandoah and Potomac Rivers will recognize a handful of places in the story where I took creative license in describing river conditions and distances. Those changes were no fault of Roger Corbett and *Virginia Whitewater* but rather mine alone, done out of necessity in constructing certain key scenes.

Retired Marine Captain Jason Haag was a vital source of information and inspiration for me in telling this story and in writing the character of Jeremy Dupree. Jason; his wife, Elizabeth; their intrepid children; and Jason's service dog, Axel, have helped countless veterans and their families struggling with PTSD and traumatic brain injuries after deployments in the wars in Iraq and Afghanistan. I am grateful to the Haag family for sharing their story with me and with the world. A series of articles I wrote about the Haags originally appeared in the Fredericksburg, Virginia, *Free Lance-Star* in 2013 and can be found in the *Free Lance-Star* archives or on my author's website, www.stevewatkinsbooks.com.

My agent, Kelly Sonnack, with the Andrea Brown Literary Agency, and my editor at Candlewick, Kaylan Adair, were as always wonderful throughout the writing and rewriting and more rewriting of *Great Falls*. They were supportive and insightful and challenged me in all the best ways.

I also couldn't have written this book without the help and the deep rivers of wisdom and generosity of my wife, Janet Watkins — nor would I have wanted to. Thanks always to my four amazing daughters — Maggie, Eva, Claire, and Lili — for making our lives so rich and so interesting, and for keeping me believing that all this truly matters.

My appreciation, as well, to Lieutenant Colonel Dave Grossman for his book *On Killing: The Psychological Cost of Learning to Kill in War and Society,* and to Karl Marlantes for his book *What It Is Like to Go to War.*

Great Falls is for all the families of those who have served. We owe them far more than we are giving in return.

RESOURCES

There are a great many resources available for families of active-duty service members and veterans who are having difficulties adjusting to life after war. As any military family will tell you, there is no one right answer or resource or direction for everyone, and no answers to post-war and post-deployment challenges come easy. Here are some resources — far from a comprehensive list — that can help. Most have links to still other organizations and resources offering information and support for military families.

Military OneSource (www.militaryonesource.mil)

The National Center for PTSD (www.ptsd.va.gov)

The National Resource Directory (www.ebenefits.va.gov /ebenefits/nrd)

Team RWB (www.teamrwb.org)

Blue Star Families (www.bluestarfam.org)

K9s for Warriors (www.k9sforwarriors.org)